SAXBY SMART
Private Detective
THE CURSE OF THE ANCIENT MASK
and Other Case Files

Simon Cheshire *Pictures by* R.W. Alley

SQUARE
FISH

Roaring Brook Press   New York

SQUARE FISH

An Imprint of Macmillan

Library of Congress Control Number: 2009933664
ISBN 978-0-312-65939-4

First published in Great Britain by Piccadilly Press Ltd.
Originally published in the United States by Roaring Brook Press
First Square Fish Edition: April 2011
Square Fish logo designed by Filomena Tuosto
Book designed by CoolKidsGraphics Inc.
www.squarefishbooks.com

10 9 8 7 6 5 4 3 2 1

AR: 5.0 / LEXILE: 730L

CASE FILE ONE:
THE CURSE OF
THE ANCIENT MASK

CHAPTER ONE

My name is Saxby Smart, and I'm a private detective. I go to St. Egbert's School, my office is in the toolshed, and these are my case files. Unlike some detectives, I don't have a sidekick, so that part I'm leaving up to you—pay attention, I'll ask questions.

My full name is Saxby Doyle Christie Chandler Ellin Allan Smart. Yes, believe it or not, I'm named after all of my dad's favorite crime writers. The Allan is from Edgar Allan Poe. I mean, even my dad wouldn't call his kid Poe Smart! Mind you, he called me Saxby Smart . . . (Saxby isn't a crime writer, by the way; Saxby is apparently a Ye Olde English name, originally pillaged from the Vikings).

Dad is a big fan of crime novels, and ever since I

could read I've worked my way through his library of great detective stories. He has an impressive collection. It was all those books that made me want to be a detective in the first place. I love them just as much as he does. Which I guess is another reason I'm beginning my case files here: to show you that I can be just as good a sleuth as Sherlock Holmes or Nancy Drew.

You might think my dad was a detective himself, but actually he's a bus driver. Not that there's anything wrong with being a bus driver. In fact, he loves being a bus driver. And I love him being a bus driver, because it means all the local bus drivers know me, and that's very useful when you're a kid detective trying to get around town following clues.

What I mean is that he only *reads* detective stories. I live them.

My mom? She programs computer games for a living. She works from home and spends all day in her office, which is the closet under the stairs. And that's all there is to say, really.

The only reason I mention my parents at all is to

let you know that I've got some. They play no part in any of my great cases, and won't be appearing much in these pages.

This is the story of my first really interesting case. Up to that point, I'd dealt with quite easy stuff: *The Adventure of the Misplaced Action Figure* or *The Case of the Eaten Cookies* are examples from my files that come to mind. But *The Curse of the Ancient Mask* was something altogether more puzzling. What's interesting is that I wrapped up the whole case using only a plastic bucket of water.

It started one very hot Saturday, while I was in my Crime Headquarters. I call it my Crime Headquarters, but really it's a shed. In my backyard. It's a small yard, and a small shed, and I have to share this shed with the lawnmower and other assorted gardening-type things. I have an old desk in there, and a cabinet full of case notes and papers. Most important of all, I have my Thinking Chair. It's a battered old leather armchair which used to be red but has worn into a sort of off-brown. I sit in it, and I put my feet up on the desk, and I gaze out the shed's Plexiglas window at the sky, and I think.

Every detective should have a Thinking Chair. I'm sure Philip Marlowe would have had things tied up in the space of a short story if only he'd had a Thinking Chair.

Anyway, on that particular very hot Saturday, I was rearranging some of my notes when there was a knock at the shed door. Its painted wooden sign, the one that says *Saxby Smart—Private Detective: KEEP OUT*, fell off with a clatter. I keep nailing it up, but I'm no good at that sort of thing, so it keeps falling off again.

The door was opened by a girl from my class at school, Jasmine Winchester. She was red and flustered from a long walk, and she fanned herself with her hands while knocking some of the grassy mud off her shoes.

"Hi, Saxby. Sorry, this dropped off your door," she said, picking up the sign.

Jasmine is a very tall girl, the sort who overtakes everyone else in height at about the age of three and never lets the rest of us catch up. I'm pretty average-looking myself—average height, average fair hair, average glasses—but Jasmine is one of those people

you can always pick out of a crowd. Mostly because she's poking out of the top of it.

"I know walking along the river looks like a shortcut," I said, "but you'd get here quicker if you stuck to the path across the park."

She stopped fanning and stared at me. "How on earth did you know I'd walked by the river?"

She looked impressed when I told her. It was a simple deduction: there was grassy mud on her shoes, she'd obviously walked some distance—because she was hot—and on a hot day, you'd only pick up mud where the ground was still damp.

"How can I help you?" I asked. I offered her my chair, and I perched on the desk (I told you there's not enough room in that shed . . .).

"Well," she said, taking a deep breath, "I can see why everyone at school says you're a good detective . . ."

"True."

". . . so I need your help to solve a mystery. My dad is cursed."

CHAPTER TWO

"My dad is an engineer at Microspek Electronics," she began. "He's worked there for years. He's head of their lab, and he helps develop new ideas. He's normally a pretty laid-back, easygoing, jokey sort of dad. But recently he's become very nervous."

"Nervous?" I said. "What about?"

"I know this sounds silly, but he thinks he's under some sort of bad luck curse, put on him by this antique mask he bought on a business trip a few months ago."

"You're right, it does sound silly."

"Yeah. But he's convinced. Ever since this mask came into the house, things have been going wrong for him at work. He's been getting into trouble with his boss."

"Why?"

"His new ideas keep getting stolen. Something must be going on at his lab. He'd worked out a brilliant way of running MP3 players from your TV remote, and then a rival company, PosiSpark, Inc., suddenly came up with the same thing. He'd also made a toaster that never burns bread, even if you forget it's on, and PosiSpark got hold of that idea, too!"

"So there must be a spy for PosiSpark working undercover at the Microspek lab."

"That's exactly what my dad's boss believes. He thinks the spy is my dad!"

"And he's not? Sorry, I have to ask," I told her.

"No," said Jasmine. "Definitely not. Dad's horrified by what's going on. And so is everyone at the lab. Every last one of them has volunteered to take lie detector tests, have their e-mails and phone records checked, and they even let them search their trash cans!" Dad's assistants are loyal to him. There's no sign whatsoever of a spy. Dad's boss still thinks Dad is the only one who could be passing such complicated info to PosiSpark, and he's just waiting to find some proof. Then Dad will be fired!"

"Hmm. No wonder your dad's feeling jumpy," I

said. I would have sat back in my Thinking Chair at this point, but Jasmine was sitting on it. So I sat back on the desk and looked thoughtful instead. "This mask. Where did he get it?"

"In Tokyo. It's an old Japanese samurai mask. He found it in a little antique shop while he was on a business trip. He buys stuff like that whenever he travels. He's not an antiques expert or anything; he just likes collecting souvenirs. The man in the shop told him there was a curse on it, but of course he thought that was nonsense. At the time. In fact, he thought it was funny and tried to scare us!"

"But if your dad now thinks the curse is real, why doesn't he just get rid of it?"

"Ah!" said Jasmine, holding up a finger like an exclamation point. "That's the sneaky part. There's Japanese writing on the back of the mask. The man in the shop translated it for him. It says that the curse stays with you even if you throw the mask away! The only way to lift it off yourself is to give it to another person."

"And since your dad believes in the curse," I said, "he doesn't want to pass it on."

"Exactly. He says he couldn't deliberately give someone an ancient curse!"

A possibility was coming to mind. The mask turns up, information begins to leak from the lab, PosiSpark snatches all the new ideas . . .

"Where exactly is the mask kept?" I asked. "At his lab?"

"You're thinking of bugs, right?" said Jasmine. "Secret agent–type cameras and stuff?"

"The possibility came to mind."

"The mask is at home, in Dad's study. He works from home sometimes. The mask is nowhere near the lab. In any case, the lab's been scanned for bugs, listening devices, hidden cameras, you name it. There's nothing. Dad's examined the mask, and searched every inch of our whole house. He's come up with precisely zero. He's convinced it's the curse."

"Well, it's a strange sort of curse, bringing such specific bad luck," I said. "Must be a very intelligent and technologically minded curse."

"The thing is," said Jasmine, "there *is* a security problem. My dad will get fired. Him buying that mask could just be a complete coincidence, but one way or another, this needs to get sorted out."

"And it will," I said. "Saxby Smart is on the case!"

A Page from My Notebook

FACT: PosiSpark is getting hold of Jasmine's dad's ideas.

FACT: His lab isn't bugged, and his assistants have been completely checked.

FACT: He bought the mask in Tokyo, and now it's sitting in his study. His bad luck began when he bought the mask.

QUESTION: How is PosiSpark getting the info?

QUESTION: Is someone lying? Is someone covering something up? Or is everyone exactly as they seem?

QUESTION: Is Jasmine right? Is the mask's arrival just a coincidence? After all, her dad simply picked it up at an antiques store. What link to his lab could there possibly be?

Unless . . . it really IS cursed . . .

CHAPTER THREE

I have to admit, I wasn't feeling as confident as I sounded. Here was a genuine, serious mystery, and, at first sight, a pretty baffling one. I had absolutely no firm clues, ideas, or theories!

My first move might have been to check out the lab. But I decided it wasn't necessary. If all those security measures hadn't found the leak, then logically the leak was probably coming from somewhere else. Besides, I somehow doubted they'd let kids into that lab!

So I went to Jasmine's house. Or rather, I got Jasmine to invite me over after school. Every day.

Naturally, Jasmine's parents had no idea that Saxby Smart, kid detective, was on the case. They assumed Jasmine had gotten a new best friend. Or else that I just kept following her home and had nowhere else to go after 3:30 in the afternoon.

As I mentioned, Jasmine is very tall, and the Winchesters, when they were all together, looked like a small herd of giraffes. Jasmine's mom is exactly like Jasmine, but even taller. Her dad is so long and thin he's like one of those distorting mirrors come to life.

Their house is quite fancy. My house has a flat roof and is shaped like a shoe box. The Winchesters' house is all chimneys and old-fashioned windows and interesting little bits of architecture.

"Nice to meet you, Saxby," said Mrs. Winchester. "Excuse me, I'm just finishing something up in the backyard." She loped away down the hall on those giraffey legs of hers. I thought she'd be in the garden pruning roses or something, but then loud clanks, bangs, and sawing noises suddenly started up outside.

"She's working on a motorcycle," explained Jasmine.

"Oh!" I said. "I wondered why she was covered in oil."

"Yup. It's not violent gardening, it's bike maintenance," said Jasmine, smiling. "All the local bikers come to her to get their motorcycles fixed. She can strip the engine of a Jujitsu T60 in twenty minutes."

"Very impressive," I agreed quietly, nodding wisely.

Jasmine showed me around the house. Nothing in particular caught my eye, clue-wise, but because Jasmine had said that her dad works from home sometimes, a couple of questions occurred to me.

"You haven't had a break-in or anything recently?" I asked.

"No," said Jasmine. "Mom put in a high-tech alarm system a couple of years ago."

"And have any repairmen come by? No, I guess your mom does all that too?"

"Right."

Another possibility had occurred to me, but Jasmine's answers had ruled it out. It had crossed my mind that someone from PosiSpark had managed to sneak into the house, but that now seemed unlikely.

The last stop on the tour was Mr. Winchester's study. I stepped in carefully, making sure I didn't disturb so much as a paper clip. It was a small room, with

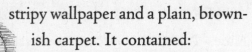

stripy wallpaper and a plain, brownish carpet. It contained:

- One large bookcase, overflowing with books.
- One set of shelves, displaying Mr. Winchester's collection of knickknacks from around the world (more on those in a minute!).
- One small desk with drawers.
- One small table holding: one coffeemaker, one set of five mugs, and one stack of filters resting on top of the coffeemaker.
- One comfy office chair, behind the desk.
- Four more chairs, stacked.

Something bothered me.

"Does your dad drink a lot of coffee?" I asked.

"I don't think so," said Jasmine, puzzled. "Why?"

"And when he works from home, he works alone?"

"Well, yes, that's why he's got this study," said Jasmine. "Nobody ever comes in here, apart from him, of course."

Suddenly, looking at the contents of the room, I made a very important discovery. From the items in the study, I could tell that Jasmine was wrong.

There was evidence here that Mr. Winchester used this room as more than a home office. Not all the time, but now and then. Can you work out what he used it for?

Mr. Winchester held meetings here. There's a coffeemaker (odd in a study, for someone who doesn't drink it much), a set of mugs, and extra chairs. Why would he keep these things unless they were used? Not used every day, because he probably wouldn't have left a big pile of filters on top of the coffeemaker if it was used all the time, would he? And the chairs wouldn't be stacked, either.

"Your dad holds meetings in here," I said. "People come here regularly."

"I never knew that," said Jasmine. "When do they happen?"

"During the school day, I presume," I said. "This makes a big difference. It establishes a link between people outside this house, and *that*!"

I pointed to the shelves above the desk. The antique mask sat among Mr. Winchester's collection of items gathered from his travels.

There was a little model of the Eiffel Tower, a snow globe from New York, and a small brass plate with a curly pattern stamped into it. ("Indian?" I asked. "Yeah," said Jasmine, "he got it in Delhi.") The mask was propped between a carved figurine of an Ancient

Egyptian god and an old china dolphin holding up a little sign that said *Souvenir of Maui*.

Jasmine got the mask down from the shelf, and we took it into the living room to get a better look at it. She was allowed to handle the collection, she explained, as long as she was careful.

The mask was rather beautiful. I turned it over in my hands—it was very heavy. It was carved out of a single piece of wood, with holes for the eyes and a kind of grille effect over the mouth. The front was painted to give it a fierce-looking face, and painted onto the back, in red, were several vertical lines of Asian writing.

"That's the inscription that sets out the curse," said Jasmine. "I bet a genius detective like you can read exactly what it says."

I blushed. "Umm . . . actually, no. Not a word. But I know someone who'll be able to translate it."

I took my cell phone out of my pocket, snapped a few pictures of the mask—front, back, side view, and so on—and sent them to my friend Izzy.

"Aarrrghhhhh!"

That was the wailing sound made by Jasmine's dad,

when he walked into the living room and spotted the mask. His face went almost the same shade of gray as the slacks he was wearing, and his tie seemed to wriggle around in shock. He picked up the mask with the very edges of his thumbs and forefingers, and held it out at arm's length as if it were a bomb.

"Let's put it back, shall we?" he said, shuddering. "We don't want to upset it!"

"Oh, Daaaad!" cried Jasmine.

Mr. Winchester wasn't listening. He was busy dabbing the sweat off his forehead with the end of his tie. "The curse is bad enough as it is. We shouldn't do anything to make it worse!"

"Mr. Winchester?" I said politely. He paused in the doorway, midstep.

"Yes?" he said quietly, as if a raised voice might make the mask explode.

"How often do you hold meetings in your study?"

"Oh, about once a month," whispered Jasmine's dad. He turned to tiptoe away, then suddenly stopped and looked at me. "How do you know about my meetings?"

I felt like saying "I know eeeeverything," all intense and spookily waving my arms about. But it would only have frightened him.

"I guess you have these meetings with a few people from your laboratory? From Microspek Electronics?" I asked.

"Yes," said Mr. Winchester. "But that's a secret! I mean, what we talk about is a secret. It's not a secret that we have meetings. Excuse me, I've got a lot on my mind at the moment."

He hurried away to put the mask back in its place.

"Does all of this tell you anything else?" said Jasmine. "Apart from the fact that my dad's normal intelligence seems to have drained away since this curse stuff started?"

"It's too early to say," I admitted.

Over the next few afternoons, I made careful notes about whatever I saw at the Winchesters' house. A lot of it turned out to be irrelevant to the case, so I won't write it all down here. But I filled several pages with information about Mr. Winchester's movements between the hours of half past three and seven p.m., about Mrs. Winchester's motorcycle repair activities, and about the workings of the Jujitsu T60 she was fixing that week.

I lurked in a few too many dark corners, I'm afraid. More than once, I made Mr. Winchester jump out of his skin and scream when he caught sight of me lurking. But once I'd explained, using my prepared cover story ("Jasmine and I are playing hide-and-seek, and I'm hiding"), and once he'd calmed down, he was okay about it.

Soon, I'd gotten as much information as I could from Jasmine's house. It was time to investigate further!

The plot was getting as thick as the "pudding" in the school cafeteria. By now, I could add some more facts to my case notes:

FACT: There is a link between the mask and the laboratory: those meetings. But! It's a very thin link! All it proves is that people from Mr. Winchester's lab have seen the mask. Does that mean anything? And if it does, what does it mean?

FACT: Mr. Winchester isn't the only one in that house good with technology. Jasmine's mom is clearly an expert in mechanics.

Is that important? Could she be the one leaking the information to PosiSpark?

FACT: Jasmine's house is a lot fancier than mine. That doesn't mean anything. It's just a fact.

CHAPTER FOUR

Isobel Moustique is one of my very best friends. She's in my class at school, and she's even smarter than me! After I texted her those pictures of the mask, I went to see her the following day.

Izzy lives a couple of streets over from me. Her room is extremely girly, with a swirly patterned rug on the mauve carpet and twinkling lights fixed in a huge spiral around the ceiling. Not the sort of room you'd normally find me hanging out in.

But don't let that fool you. There's nothing pink and fluffy about Izzy herself; she gets top grades for everything at school, and she knows enough facts to fill an encyclopedia (and then still have enough facts left over to create a really difficult quiz). Believe me, that girl is sharper than a freshly sharpened needle in a sharp needle store!

"Saxby Smart," she said, giving me that lopsided smile of hers. "I got your texts. Need my help again, do you?"

"Ooooh," I said, doing a quick roll of the eyes, my mouth set in a silly *O* shape. "I just thought you might like the chance to catch up to me on this one. You know, see if you can come to the same conclusions as quickly as I did. That sort of thing."

"Catch up to you?" said Izzy, with an expression that made her look like a tiger about to pounce. Well, a friendly tiger, anyway. "Saxby, I doubt you've come to the same conclusions about this mask as I have."

"Ooooh, really? Here are my conclusions," I said. "The mask is Japanese. It is very old; it was worn by a samurai warrior. From its weight I'd say it was made of teak or a similar hardwood. Not environmentally friendly, but then, they didn't have global warming in the eighteenth century, did they? And it has a Japanese inscription on the back, which goes on about a curse that will befall anyone who blah, blah, blah. I think that's about it." I folded my arms and grinned at her.

"Almost totally wrong," she said. She grinned back at me, looking more tiger-like than ever.

"WHAT?" I sputtered.

Izzy had done her research. She'd checked books, she'd checked the Internet, and she'd checked her vast brain for facts about masks. On her computer screen, she opened up the photos I'd sent her and pointed out three things:

1. The mask was made from pine, or a similar soft wood that's light in weight. You could tell this from the patterns you could see where the wood had been cut.

2. The face on the mask had nothing to do with samurai warriors. It was based on a demon found in traditional Thai theater.

3. However, the writing on the back of the mask was indeed Japanese. It translated as "Power plastic wobble television, blue teeth microwave paint circuit between electric light."

For a second or two I stood there, on Izzy's curly patterned rug, completely silent. I was very embarrassed.

"WHAT?" I repeated.

"It all checks out," said Izzy. "That mask is a fake.

I think it's nothing more than a cheap souvenir. It looks like Jasmine's dad simply got duped into buying a rather badly made imitation. It's not even that old. You wouldn't find the Japanese characters for 'television' or 'plastic' painted on a genuine antique, would you?"

Unexpected as Izzy's findings were, there was no disputing them. Izzy is never wrong.

"Your info is as vital as ever, Iz," I said sadly.

"Where does this leave your investigation?" Izzy asked.

"I'm not sure," I told her.

I gave her a cheery wave. She went back to her books. I went back to my shed. I sat in my Thinking Chair, propped my feet up on my desk, and fixed my face into the special detectivey expression I'd been practicing in the bathroom mirror: eyes narrowed, one eyebrow raised, everything else showing steely determination.

I thought about Izzy's first point. The one about the mask being made of a soft wood, like pine. How could I have gotten that so wrong?

And then it struck me! There was a clear difference between what I had thought, based on handling the mask, and what Izzy could tell, by looking at its photos. And this difference meant something very important! Something about how the mask was constructed. Have you figured it out too?

The mask had to be made of something else, in addition to the wood. To me, it felt quite heavy, remember? But Izzy made it clear that the wood it was made from should have been quite light. So the mask *must* have been made of something else *as well*. Something out of sight!

This was getting interesting! I thought about Izzy's second point, the one about the mask having nothing to do with samurai warriors. It would be very strange for a Japanese souvenir, bought in Japan, to have gotten a detail like that wrong. After all, if I took a day trip to

Chicago, souvenirs of the place wouldn't include the Statue of Liberty or the Golden Gate Bridge. No matter who had made them, or where they'd been made, they'd include the Sears Tower, Wrigley Field, and so on and so on.

Which made me wonder: was it *really* just a cheap, touristy souvenir after all?

And this made me think about Izzy's third point, the one about the writing on the back of the mask.

Immediately, another important deduction snapped into place! I checked my notebook, and Izzy's translation. Something was staring out at me from the words of that painted inscription, something about *who* had made the mask.

Whoever made the mask *could not speak Japanese.* That inscription was not a curse. Well, obviously. But it wasn't anything—it was a load of nonsense! The person who painted those Japanese characters onto the mask clearly had no idea what they meant!

And *then*, another important deduction came from that! I almost fell off my Thinking Chair, I was so impressed with my cleverness.

Let's take a close look at that nonsense writing. It said: "Power plastic wobble television, blue teeth microwave paint circuit between electric light."

Now, whoever painted those words—this person who couldn't speak Japanese—must have copied those characters from *somewhere*. They *were* actual Japanese characters; they'd simply been thrown together like a bunch of junk.

So! There was something hugely significant in the words *themselves*. There was a clear connection here between the mask, whoever made it, and Mr. Winchester's troubles at Microspek Electronics. For the first time, looking at the words used in that inscription, I could establish that the arrival of the mask did seem to be linked to Mr. Winchester's work. How?

Most of the words were connected with *electronics*—Mr. Winchester's line of work! Terms like "television," "microwave," "power," and "electric light" were words you might expect to see when reading about electronics.

I sat in my Thinking Chair, brain zipping along faster than a bike without brakes on a very steep hill. This case was coming together!

Okay, so whoever painted that inscription—this person who couldn't speak Japanese—copied the words from something *written* in Japanese, that was *probably* all about electronics.

This was what we detectives call "circumstantial evidence." It wasn't actual *proof*.

Here's an example: proof is when you have a photo of that low-down rat-of-the-classroom Harry Lovecraft stealing your pencil case, and you have three witnesses who saw that low-down rat Harry Lovecraft steal your pencil case. That's proof. In a case like that, there's no way that low-down rat Harry Lovecraft could wriggle out of it, or pretend it wasn't him. You'd have proof.

Anyway, what I'd been able to deduce about the mask was not proof. The mask *could* still have been an el cheapo tourist souvenir. But it didn't seem *likely*. The writing on the mask *could* simply have been copied from the manual for someone's new camcorder. But it didn't seem *likely*, not when you put all the other clue-type ingredients into the pot. The mask was very fishy. Fishier than a fish shop that's just had a fresh delivery of fish!

The next morning at school, Jasmine hurried over to me. She looked very worried.

"Saxby!" she said. "Have you made any progress on the case?"

"Yes, some," I replied, hoping that some was enough. It wasn't.

"My dad's in huge trouble," said Jasmine. "Microspek's rival, PosiSpark, has just announced a new line of cell phones with built-in photo printers. That was what my dad was working on. PosiSpark's stolen his idea again! Dad's boss went purple with rage. He told my dad that if this security leak isn't stopped by Friday, he'll be suspended from his job."

"That's not very fair," I said.

"Fair or not, it's happening," said Jasmine. "Saxby, you've got to do something—and fast!"

FACT: The mask is a fake. It's not old, it's not even Japanese.

QUESTION: How'd it get into a Tokyo tourist shop? And why?

FACT: It's <u>likely</u> (not certain, but likely) that the mask was made by someone with access to lots of stuff written about electronics (including stuff written in Japanese).

QUESTION: Can I get to the bottom of this by Friday?

CHAPTER FIVE

For a couple of days, things at school kept me away from my shed and my Thinking Chair. Our class had to prepare a set of science demonstrations for Parents' Night, and my other best friend, Muddy Whitehouse, and I got stuck doing stuff about levers and pulleys. He's brilliant with that sort of thing, but I can't tell a fulcrum from a plate of spaghetti!

It wasn't until Wednesday that I could properly get back on the trail of the info leak. Luckily, I'd been able to get some thinking done, and I'd reached some possible conclusions. These possible conclusions now needed to be backed up with some solid facts.

I e-mailed Izzy again. I asked her to come up with some general research on the electronics industry—newspaper clippings, background info on Microspek and PosiSpark, things like that. Anything that might have a bearing on the case. She's much better at doing those kinds of things than I am. She's very thorough—I skip stuff.

In the meantime, I returned to Jasmine's house after school. There were some more questions I needed to ask. More to the point, I needed to slim down my list of suspects. And quickly!

What was really confusing me in this case was that the motive (*why* the crime happened), opportunity (*when* the crime happened), and method (*how* the crime happened) all seemed to be at odds with one another. As I walked over to Jasmine's house, flipping back and forth through my notebook, I began to realize that this mystery couldn't be solved without some fresh evidence turning up. You see, there were a couple of BUTs here.

BUT No. 1: The only people who could be leaking information were the Winchesters themselves, or the people at Microspek—BUT! They had no motive. Mr. Winchester's boss was confident there was no spy in the lab, remember? (Besides, it seems to me that if you're going to pay a spy huge wads of cash, you might as well simply hire the people you're spying on. It would probably be cheaper.)

BUT No. 2: The only people who *did* have a motive for the leak worked at PosiSpark—BUT! I had nothing whatsoever to tell me about their *opportunity* or *method*. Sure, the mask was highly suspicious, but what was the link between the mask and PosiSpark? It was a souvenir bought in Japan! What link could there possibly be?

I walked home, intending to go straight to my Thinking Chair.

CHAPTER SIX

As I turned the corner onto my street, Izzy was arriving with a box full of papers.

"Here," she said, heaving the box into my arms. "I printed out the info you wanted on the electronics industry."

I stared into the box. It was full to the top, and very heavy.

"It'll take me *weeks* to sort through all this," I said sadly.

"You're telling me," said Izzy. "I've got three more boxes at home. I'll get my mom to drive me over with the rest of it later. I thought you'd want to get started straightaway. Seeing as you have . . ." She checked her watch. " . . . roughly forty-eight hours before Jasmine's dad gets suspended and

41

your reputation as a detective goes down the drain."

There was NO WAY that was happening. I wasn't about to let anyone else be the world's greatest kid detective!

I got started at once. The stuff Izzy had gotten hold of could be separated into three piles: newspaper articles, sales information, and trade press. The sales information was facts and figures about Microspek and PosiSpark products, that sort of thing. The trade press was news and info put together for people who work in electronics—web forum entries, news blogs, or exciting, gripping reads such as *Electronic Monthly* magazine and *Circuit Board Bulletin*.

I gathered together piles on top of the desk in my shed. One by one, I went through every sheet in the box. Just as I was getting to the bottom sheet, Izzy arrived with the other three boxes. One by one, I went through every piece of paper in those boxes too.

Ohhh, it was *so* boring . . . ! Most of what I read went further over my head than a rocket disappearing into space. After a couple of hours I could barely remember my name, let alone the functions of a P238 integrated circuit micro-pudding mango whatsit, or whatever it was.

But then I came across a very interesting newspaper clipping. I sat up straight, blinking and alert. After a quick reminder to myself of what my name was, I set it to one side, on a fourth pile marked AHA!

Apart from minor interruptions (for going to sleep, going to school, going to the bathroom, and eating), I kept on digging through those boxes until eight the following night. By then, there were four items in my AHA! pile.

Here they are. See if you can spot the clues I got from them. Some of the info here is not relevant to the case, but some of it is absolutely vital! There are important deductions to be made about the guilty party . . .

ITEM 1: Newspaper clipping from *The Daily Shout*, dated nine months ago.

TECHNO FIRMS FACE BLEAK FUTURE

Wall Street spending on electronics has nosedived.

"People only want the most useful gadgets," said Keith Bletch, 37, of the Shopping Statistics Survey, which today revealed its findings on the electronics industry. "Nobody wants junk that doesn't work after five minutes, or that isn't eco-friendly," he added.

Companies like Microspek, Electro-World, and PosiSpark are facing a bleak future, unless they can create new products that suit today's needs.

"We're sure we'll pull through," said Bill Plum, president of Microspek. "My lab team is second to none!"

ITEM 2: Printout of www.PosiSpark.com, from the *What We Do* section.

What We Do

PosiSpark, Inc. is the world's most exciting and dynamic company in the electronics field. Our products define simplicity and usefulness in the 21st century. Some examples of our brand-new designs include:

PosiSpark **MP25 Projection Modules™**

A line of handheld devices for a truly portable cinematic experience. Upload photos, movies, and TV shows, then project them onto a blank wall like a flashlight. *[Blank wall, darkened room, and good eyesight required.]*

PosiSpark **Hidden Sound Systems™**

A range of metal plates that can be built into furniture, to act as either speakers or microphones. Listen to music through your bureau, or talk on your cell phone using your coffee table. *[Super-long-life "Ultra-power" PosiSpark battery pack™ with 2-year guarantee required. Furniture not included.]*

PosiSpark Pre-Boil Kettles™

A range of kitchen kettles that switch themselves on the moment you think about having a cup of tea. Simply wear the PosiSpark Brainwave Hat™ at all times, and as soon as you think about tea, the hat transmits your desire to the kettle. *[Water and electricity supply required. PosiSpark Brainwave Hat™ sold separately.]*

ITEM 3: Article from *Electronics Industry Today* magazine, dated eight months ago.

COMPETITION WINNERS

We've had a flood of entries for our *Me and My Interesting Collection* photo competition, so a big thanks to all twelve of you! We printed the six finalists in the last issue, and our readers' votes have now picked the winners!

FIRST PRIZE

(a T852R circuit board):

Miss Daphne Spottswood

Integrated Keyboards, Inc.

For her photo of her office, with her enormous collection of cake pans.

SECOND PRIZE

(a selection of interface cables):

Mr. P. L. Smith

The Electrical Spare Parts Supply Co.

For his picture of himself surrounded by his collection of postcards from Caribbean beach resorts.

THIRD PRIZE

(*Electronics Industry Today* subscription):

Mr. Kenneth Winchester

Microspek Electronics

For his photo of his dense home office, featuring his collection of knickknacks from around the world.

We hope this fabulous competition has proved once and for all that the electronics industry is not at all boring.

ITEM 4: Printout of the personal blog of Dr. Hans Upp, professor in applied electronics at the University School of Colleges.

March 7

Arrived in Tokyo for fascinating conference, "Electronics: Perspectives in Sales and Function." Hotel has lost my suitcase.

March 8

Conference begins. A lot to pack into two days! Met a number of old friends, including Daphne Spottswood, Kenneth Winchester, and the team from the PosiSpark labs. Hardly time to talk, so much to pack in. Hotel can't find my suitcase.

March 9

Conference runs late. Everyone flying home soon. Winchester frantic to find quality souvenir of Japan before flight. PosiSpark gang suggests a shop to him. Nice how business rivals can get along so well. Hotel has found and destroyed suitcase, thinking it had been abandoned.

March 10

Arrive home. Smell awful due to lack of clean clothes. Have a bath and buy new suitcase.

At eight p.m., the mystery was solved! Now I knew it all! I had worked out *exactly* what had been going on all this time. Have you?

CHAPTER SEVEN

I called Jasmine and asked her to arrange a meeting in her living room after school on Friday. I told her that the mystery was solved and that her dad's job was safe.

She asked me why I couldn't just tell her all about it on the phone right then. I explained that all great detectives gather everyone together at the end to reveal the truth.

So, after school, five people assembled at the Winchesters' house: me, Jasmine, Mr. Winchester, Mrs. Winchester, and Bill Plum, the president of Microspek. Bill Plum was so short and round that he was having trouble sitting on the Winchesters' sofa. His head, with a face that seemed to be permanently enraged, looked like a cherry plonked on top of a sponge cake.

"What's wrong with this sofa, Winchester?" he mumbled.

Mrs. Winchester was busy rubbing the oil stains off her hands with a damp cloth. Mr. Winchester simply sat with his head in his hands, looking doomed. Jasmine kept looking at me with an expression on her face that said, "Why did you bring over a bucket of water?"

If I'd been one of those detectives in my dad's crime novels, I would have been standing in front of a roaring fireplace, while thunder and lightning stormed outside a country mansion (because that's what they always seem to do). However, in reality, we weren't anywhere near a country mansion. So I had to stand in front of the Winchesters' unlit gas fire instead.

The bucket of water that sat beside me was there for a very important reason.

Meanwhile, I picked up the mask from the coffee table in front of me.

I cleared my throat noisily. Everyone fell silent.

"Hello," I said.

Now that I was standing in front of them all, I suddenly realized I'd never actually done this before. I'd read scenes like this plenty of times, but I'd never had to be in one. So I made it up as I went along.

"I'll make one thing clear right now," I said. "This mask is not cursed."

"Oh yeah?" mumbled Mr. Winchester.

"This mask," I continued, "is not an antique, either. But it is this mask that has been leaking information to PosiSpark."

"What?" sputtered Bill Plum. "Are you serious?"

"I mean it," I said. "All the information that Posi-Spark has stolen came to them through this mask."

"Because it's cursed," muttered Mr. Winchester.

"No," I said patiently. "Because PosiSpark made it themselves." I held up the clipping from *The Daily Shout.* "We know that the electronics industry is going through hard times. New ideas are the key to success. PosiSpark would love to get its hands on Mr. Winchester's brilliant ideas for Microspek. They have clear motives for stealing them."

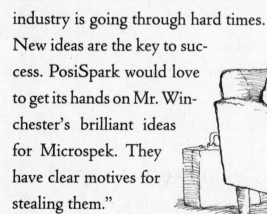

I held up a pointed finger to make sure they paid special attention here. "However! PosiSpark knows they can't place bugs or spies in the Microspek lab without being discovered. Even this house has been checked."

"Correct!" barked Bill Plum. "I won't be fooled by nonsense like that!"

"Right," I said. "So. What can PosiSpark do?"

"Nothing!" cried Bill Plum.

"No," I said. "They can read the *Electronics Industry Today*

magazine." I held up the article about competition winners. "Mr. Winchester likes to think that the business meetings in his study are a big secret. But in fact, the whole world knows about them."

Now it was Mr. Winchester's turn to sputter "What?"

"You see," I said, "printed in *Electronics Industry Today* was a picture of everything in Mr. Winchester's study. He sent it in as his entry in an extremely boring photo contest. A picture of his whole study—shelves, chairs, everything. Think about it. I took one look at that study, and I deduced there were meetings there. The bad guys at PosiSpark could have done exactly the same thing. They could have looked at the picture, seen the contents of the room, and known that Mr. Winchester held meetings in it."

"And so they made that mask?" said Jasmine. "I don't see the connection, if the mask isn't bugged."

"Microspek was wrong. It *is* bugged, sort of," I said. "But not in any way you'd normally think. That's why they completely missed it. The whole mask works like a microphone."

I held up the printout of PosiSpark's Web site. "As

soon as I found out about these PosiSpark Hidden Sound Systems, it became obvious. Notice how these systems need plenty of power. If they were going to listen in on Mr. Winchester's meetings, they'd need a very, very good power supply, one that would last for months, maybe even years. The mask is made of a light wood. But it's heavy. The difference? Batteries! Super-long-life "Ultra-power" PosiSpark battery packs built inside the mask, completely undetectable unless you tear the mask apart."

Jasmine was staring at me slightly bug-eyed. The rest of them were staring at me slightly bug-eyed, too.

"But how did PosiSpark expect to get that mask into my dad's study?" said Jasmine. "He just bought it in a shop."

"Ah, but not any shop," I said. This time, I pointed to the printout of Dr. Hans Upp's blog. "It was partly luck. From the magazine article, PosiSpark knew that Mr. Winchester buys souvenirs when he travels, and from the photo they knew what kinds of things he liked. They knew he was going to Japan. They made the mask, and then they needed to get him to buy it!"

"Couldn't they have just given it to him?" said Jasmine. "As a present or something?"

"They could, yes," I agreed. "But think how suspicious *that* would look. PosiSpark gives him a gift, then PosiSpark starts getting hold of his ideas. You'd spot a connection at once. No, they had to make your dad think *he* was choosing *it*, not the other way around. And this was where they had a stroke of luck. Time at the conference was very short. Mr. Winchester made it clear that he wanted to go and get a souvenir quickly, before everyone had to fly home. So what do those lovely, helpful guys from PosiSpark do? They tell him where there's a nearby store. *They* tell *him*."

"I see," said Jasmine quietly, a smile spreading across her face. "All they had to do was place the mask, bribe the shopkeeper to tell Dad all about a curse, and bingo."

"Exactly," I said. "Your dad buys the mask, brings it home, starts having some bad luck, remembers the curse, normal sensible attitude to curses goes out the window, can't make the connection with PosiSpark, and so on. You know, that might explain why the mask wasn't accurately Japanese. PosiSpark couldn't be sure they'd get it into your dad's hands on that trip. They might have had to wait for the next one, somewhere else, so they may have made the mask fairly general-looking, to fit into several possible overseas locations."

"Makes sense," said Jasmine, nodding.

"It makes no sense at all!" exclaimed Bill Plum. "A devious, underhanded, nasty little scheme like that? The explanation's much simpler. Winchester here is selling secrets to PosiSpark! I've had enough of this nonsense. Winchester, you're suspended!"

"Wait!" I cried. "What if I could prove that the mask is one giant microphone? Would that convince you? I'm going to switch it off by dropping it into this bucket of water. If I'm wrong, then nothing will happen. If I'm right, the batteries inside it will short-circuit, and there'll be a spark."

I picked up the mask and held it over the bucket. There was absolute silence in the room. A stab of nerves hit me. IF I'm right . . .

I let the mask go. It plopped into the water. Instantly, there was a flash, a sharp crackling sound, and a smell like burned toast.

"Ah," said Bill Plum. "Winchester, you're not suspended after all. I'm going to call the police."

"You should be quick," I said. "PosiSpark will have just overheard everything I said. They might start covering things up!"

Bill Plum struggled wildly to get up off the sofa, his arms and legs flapping. Mr. Winchester bounded to his feet and starting skipping about, emitting squeals of delight. He kissed Mrs. Winchester, he kissed Jasmine, he kissed Bill Plum.

Mrs. Winchester helped Bill Plum up onto his feet, and he scrambled out of the room as fast as his tiny legs would carry him, dialing into his cell phone. He scrubbed at his cheek where Mr. Winchester had kissed him.

"Oh, joy!" squeaked Mr. Winchester. "Oh, I'm so relieved! Oh, Saxby, you're a genius! Oh, how wonderful everything is! Oh, joy! Oh, happiness!"

Oh, good grief! Apparently, he didn't stop jabbering and skipping around for two days straight. I think I preferred him when he believed in the curse!

Anyway, Jasmine told everyone at school the

whole story next Monday morning, and I felt like a hero. At the end of the day, I returned to my toolshed, and my notebooks, and my Thinking Chair, and I sat for a while and thought.

Case closed.

CASE FILE TWO:
THE MARK OF THE PURPLE HOMEWORK

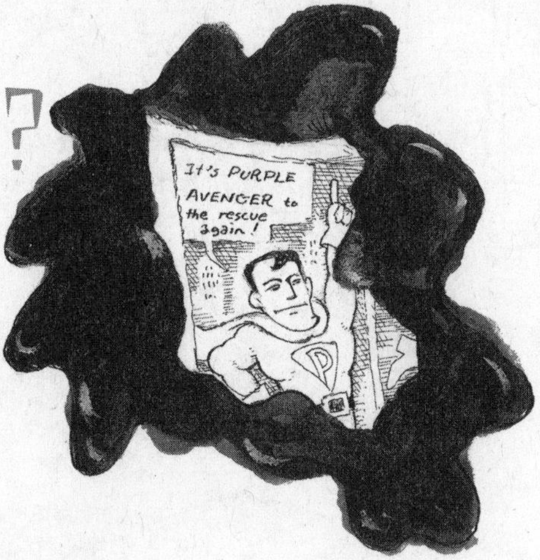

CHAPTER ONE

I don't like dogs. They're grubby, noisy, jump-up-and-downy animals. They walk around fields in their bare paws and then slob out on the sofa! Yuck!

However, strange as it seems, it was a dog named Humphrey that provided the vital link in the chain of clues in a mystery I like to call *The Mark of the Purple Homework*.

Humphrey isn't just a dog. He is a *big* dog. A huge, heavy, bloodhound-floppy-eared-wrinkly-skinned thing. And he has a habit of sitting right in front of the door to my shed.

He belongs to a boy in my class, Jeremy Sweetly, who lives right across the street. Jeremy absolutely adores this slobbery great lump of a dog, and to this day I have no idea why. Humphrey can't do any tricks, has no training whatsoever, and spends most of his time sniffing around for food. The only thing he *is* good at is drooling. That dog could be World Slobbering Champion.

On the morning of March 16th, I was hurrying out to my shed to collect my notes on the case of *The Tomb of Death*. I was already running late, and would have to jog to school. And there was Humphrey, with his butt parked right in front of the shed door.

I whistled. I spoke nicely. I tugged at his collar. He wouldn't move. I yelled. I shouted. There was no way I could get the shed door open with that dopey hound plonked there.

I went over to Jeremy's house. "He's outside my shed again!" I cried.

"Sorry," said Jeremy with a weak smile. "There must be something in there he likes the smell of."

"Isn't there any way to keep him safe in your yard?"

"He keeps getting out. He likes to wander around. He's a very intelligent dog."

"Really," I said flatly.

Jeremy followed me back to the shed. He made one

little "tkk-tkk" noise, and Humphrey lumbered to his feet (or rather his paws) and loped after his owner. I stepped over the puddle of drool outside my shed and collected my notes.

Jeremy Sweetly. He's a nice guy. Nicey-nice. Too nice for his own good. He is, to be brutally honest, the St. Egbert's School resident doofus. He shows no embarrassment whatsoever at admitting he carries around a miniature teddy bear.

Don't get me wrong, I like him. Everybody does. He's so kind hearted he makes social workers look like an evil villain's henchmen! But he was never exactly the first one with his hand up in class—"Ohhh, me, me, I know!"—even when he knew the answer.

The basic nature of Jeremy Sweetly would prove highly significant in this case.

I was almost late for school that day. Running like mad, I nearly collided with the janitor's ladder on the way in (he was fixing the leaky roof over the bathroom).

Jeremy was almost late, too, probably because he'd spent several minutes getting Humphrey back into his house, and then several more minutes saying "Bye-bye-my-wittle-doggie," etc., etc.

That day marked the official launch of this year's School Essay Challenge. Every spring, all the local schools take part in a competition; we all write illustrated essays on whatever topic happens to appeal to us. There's a winner in each school (who gets a twenty-dollar bookstore gift card, or something like that), and the winning essays get judged by all the principals. The overall winner gets a big prize, like a bike or a game system.

"This year's prize," said Mrs. Penzler, our homeroom teacher, "is a laptop."

"Oooh," said the class. Everyone in class except me,

that is. I made a sort of wheezy noise because I was still out of breath from running to school. "I'm so out of shape!" I gasped to myself.

Mostly, everyone keeps their essay topic a secret until it's time to hand them in. I don't know why. We just do. It makes for some fun gossip. But, me being a detective, I tend to work out what most people are doing for their essay within the first week.

All eyes were on Jeremy Sweetly. He was the hot favorite to win this year: he had come in second two years ago, and won the overall prize last year with a very interesting piece entitled *The Life Story of My Dad*.

For a few days, pretty much the entire class spent lunchtime sneaking around the school library and downloading stuff in the computer lab. I saw Jeremy a couple of times in the local records section at the public library and talking to the people who'd been living next door to the school since roughly the beginning of time. I'd decided to enter a certain case file entitled *The Curse of the Ancient Mask*.

I swapped titles with my two friends, Izzy Moustique and George "Muddy" Whitehouse, partly because we were best friends and partly because there was no way Muddy would be able to keep his essay a secret for long. He'd get too excited and blab.

Izzy's essay was going to be called *Global Warming and Sun/Cosmic Ray Activity* and would be packed with diagrams. Muddy was doing a how-to thing about making your own self-propelled bicycle.

"Have you worked out what he's doing yet?" whispered Muddy, when we spotted Jeremy coming out of the busy school office one afternoon with a bundle of notes under his arm.

"Hmm," I said. "Well, he wasn't there because he got into trouble. Jeremy Sweetly does not get into trouble. Sooooo, yes, having observed him over the past few days, I think I have a good idea of what he's writing about."

Have you worked it out?

"He's writing about the school," I said. "More likely, the history of the school. He's been looking up local records and talking to people who'd know about that stuff."

Muddy whistled with admiration. "Now *that* is a real teacher-pleaser," he said, scratching his knee and sending a little shower of dried mud to the floor.

"I think our Jeremy's going to do it again," I said, nodding.

I was completely wrong!

The following morning, a crime came to light. Mrs. Penzler gave us half an hour to work on our essays before starting the first lesson. We all reached into our school bags and pulled out our various notebooks and printouts. Jeremy Sweetly pulled out the CD he'd stored all his research on.

The disk was ruined! It had been coated in a thick purple substance that had dried all hard and rubbery. Slapped in the middle of this stuff was a slip of paper, neatly cut from some magazine, on which was printed in large letters:

YOU HAVE BEEN STRUCK
BY THE PURPLE AVENGER!
HAHA!

He held up the CD between thumb and forefinger, speechless with shock. At that moment, the entire class gave what would become, during this case, the first in a trio of loud gasps.

CHAPTER TWO

I quickly made a mental list of suspects. The list read:

• Everyone!

The whole class had a motive. The whole *school* had a motive! We *all* knew that Jeremy Sweetly had the best chance of winning the competition. Anyone might have done it, in order to knock the favorite out of the running.

Which didn't exactly make things easy. As soon as the entire class had stopped gasping, they looked right at me. This was clearly a case for my detective skills. (At least, I *hope* that's why they looked right at me . . .)

"Aren't the files still on a computer, Jeremy?" asked Mrs. Penzler. She hadn't gasped. Mrs. Penzler was a no-nonsense sort of teacher. Whatever she wore always looked like it was stiff as a board, and she had strange, smoked glasses that completely hid her eyes.

"I transferred everything off the school computer to this disk yesterday," wailed Jeremy, "and I was going to back it up on my home computer tonight. I never kept the hard copies of my notes. I've lost them all!"

"Oh," said Mrs. Penzler, sadly. For Mrs. Penzler, this was showing great sympathy. A sad "oh" was her equivalent of rushing over and giving him a hug. "You'll never have time to redo it before the essays are due," she said.

Jeremy's lower lip started fluttering like a leaf in a hurricane. Meanwhile, my attention was drawn to the back of the classroom. My list of suspects might have included everyone, but there was one person who was sure to be at the top of it: that low-down rat Harry Lovecraft. Sure enough, he was sitting there, at his desk, smirking evilly to himself.

After the bell rang for recess, Muddy and I went over to Jeremy Sweetly's desk. Once we'd given him a tissue and he'd given his nose a good blow, he started to feel a bit better.

"I'm out of the competition now," he said.

"Maybe you could scrape that stuff off the disk?"

said Muddy. "I once dropped my alarm clock down the toilet by mistake, and it still works. Mostly."

"That's not really the same thing, Muddy," I said. "And how on earth did you . . . ? Hmm, never mind."

I examined the ruined disk. What *was* that purple stuff? From the way it formed a sort of gloopy shape, it had obviously been some kind of thick liquid, which had then dried to form a rubbery, slightly sticky layer. The piece of paper had been pressed into it while it was still wet. On closer inspection, the paper was from a comic strip—there was half a face and a bit of speech bubble.

"So who's The Purple Avenger?" asked Muddy.

"I'll give you one guess," I said. I raised my voice, to make sure that low-down rat Harry Lovecraft heard me. He was passing us, on his way out of the classroom.

"Don't look at me, Smart," he said. "If Sweetly here can't look after his stuff, that's his own problem."

"I saw you smirking!" I told him. "I know you're behind this!"

"Not guilty," said Harry. If he was any slimier, he'd have been a frog. Harry Lovecraft is the only person

I've ever met who could play football in February and not get mud on his shorts. He has shiny black hair cut in perfectly straight lines, and shiny black shoes, and weaselly eyes. He has the sort of face that demands a thin, twirly mustache, like a bad guy in an old movie. The guy just oozes snottiness.

"Accidents happen," he said, grinning.

"Yes," I said, "convenient accidents that put the competition's front runner out of the picture."

"Oh yessss," said Harry, pretending to be surprised. "I hadn't thought of that."

And off he smarmed. Ewww!

"Don't you worry, Jeremy," I said. "Saxby Smart is on the case! That low-down rat won't get away with it."

"No, no, no," said Jeremy. "He's right. It was an accident. I don't need you to investigate anything, really."

"Don't be stupid," said Muddy. "That disk was wrecked on purpose."

"I'm sure something just tipped over into my bag. That's all. Just an unfortunate accident. Honest," said Jeremy. "It's probably jam. My mom probably knocked a jar over and it all plopped in. Never mind."

I frowned. "You don't think it was sabotage?"

"Oh, no, no."

"Then how do you explain the note from The Purple Avenger?" I asked.

"It must have been torn out of the superhero comic I was reading. Look!"

And out of his backpack he produced a recent issue of a comic book that was indeed entitled *The Purple Avenger (Trouble in the Skies! The Avenger Faces DOOOOOM!)*. It certainly looked ratty, all wrinkled and ripped at the corners.

"Oh," said Muddy. "Well, maybe it was an accident after all."

But I was highly suspicious! From my examination of the disk, I knew that the piece of paper hadn't simply been torn out of Jeremy's comic book. How?

I knew because that paper, stuck to the disk, was neatly cut. If it had been accidentally torn from the comic book, it would have had rough edges.

"So, Jeremy," I said, "you're convinced it was an accident?"

"Must have been," said Jeremy quickly. "I put the disk in my backpack yesterday, straight out of one of the computers in the computer lab. It never left the bag. I swear!"

"Do you mind if I take a look inside the bag?" I asked.

"No problem," said Jeremy. He emptied it onto his desk. There was:

- One school notebook.
- Two paperback books.
- One pencil case.
- One ratty Purple Avenger comic book.
- One miniature teddy bear named Norman.

He put them in a line, all neat and tidy (well, except the comic book!). I looked inside the bag. Empty. None of the yucky stuff that always seems to pop up inside backpacks!

"And the disk hasn't left the bag?" I asked. "Not once?"

"Absolutely not," said Jeremy.

I *knew* he was mistaken. The disk *must* have been taken out at some point.

How did I know?

The contents of the bag, and the bag itself, were clean. If that purple stuff had gone into the bag as Jeremy thought, it would have ended up on more than just the disk. Therefore, the disk must have been removed. Which made it all the more likely that it had been deliberately ruined.

"Well, I'm so glad we've sorted all that out," said Jeremy. "Just my bad luck! Oh well, there's always next year."

"Do you mind if I keep the disk?" I said.

"Not at all," said Jeremy, handing it over. "It's no good to anyone now."

He gathered up his stuff and hurried away.

"So," said Muddy, "looks like there's no case for Saxby Smart after all."

"On the contrary!" I said, turning the disk over and over in my hands. "He's hiding something."

"Oh, come on!" said Muddy. "If he thought it was sabotage, he'd have said so! The only reason he'd start covering it up was if he'd done it himself! And that's just plain maaaaad!" He made a twirling motion with his finger and pulled a dopey face.

"Hmm," I said. "Just plain mad . . ."

FACT: Jeremy Sweetly _is_ covering something up.

QUESTION: _Why???_ He's the only one in school who would _not_ have a motive for ruining his work!

FACT: Harry Lovecraft is a low-down rat. (_But_ like any good detective, I must be fair. So far, there's nothing linking him to the disk.)

FACT: Even if Harry Lovecraft _didn't_ do it, that still leaves a couple hundred possible suspects... Including all my friends!

I'VE GOT TO FIGURE OUT THREE THINGS:

1. _Why_ Jeremy would want to lie.
2. What that purple stuff is—this could be an important lead.
3. If there are any other clues to be found from that disk.

CHAPTER THREE

There *was* another clue to be found from the disk. That message from The Purple Avenger—*You have been struck* . . . —on closer examination looked like it had been printed separately on top of the cut-out piece of comic book. If I could trace the computer it had been printed from, that might give me a lead.

It was a pretty weak clue, as far as clues go, but it was the only one I had. I went to Izzy Moustique's house after school, and explained the problem.

"That's a pretty weak clue, as far as clues go," she said.

"I know," I grumbled.

She took a quick scan of the disk, for her records, and held it under the light of the pink-shaded lamp on her flower-stickered desk.

"I doubt there'll be much information to get from this," she said. And when a brainbox like Izzy says something like that, you might as well give up. "Could Saxby Smart have met his match?"

"Certainly not," I said with a sly smile. "Every problem has a solution." I rubbed my chin in a particularly detective-like way. "Why go to the trouble of creating the note? Why not just destroy the disk?"

"Exactly," said Izzy. "The note shows that the damage can't possibly have been accidental."

"It's as if this Purple Avenger person is gloating," I said. "Ha ha, you can't catch me. By the way, what do you think that purple stuff is?"

"I've come up with some possibilities," said Izzy. She picked at a bit of the stuff, and it snapped off with a rubbery twang. She swung around on her brightly cushioned swivel chair and grabbed a couple of printouts on her desk.

"It's not any type of paint," she said, running a finger down the page. Most of her fingers were sporting chunky rings with fake jewels today. "And, as you say, it must have started as liquid and then set. There are three things it might be . . . "

And they were:

1. A type of heavy-duty sealant, used for making things waterproof.
2. A certain glue used by people who install kitchens, for sticking countertops together, that sort of thing.
3. An insulator, normally used in very small amounts inside computers, to protect the most delicate circuits.

"And is Jeremy Sweetly likely to do any of those things?" said Izzy, shrugging her shoulders. "He's not exactly into stuff like kitchen installation, is he?"

"No," I said. "You wouldn't find them in many . . . Wait!" A memory flashed across my brain. A memory from that morning, rushing to school! "Wait!" I cried. "I know what it might be! It *is* one of those three possibilities!"

Have you spotted it?

82

"It's a waterproof sealant whatsit!" I cried. "The janitor was fixing the leaky roof this morning. I bet he used something like that."

"So the disk was damaged at school," said Izzy. "Not at Jeremy's house."

"Most probably."

Of course, this didn't help me work out who had damaged the disk, but it gave me an important starting point. I left the disk with Izzy, thanked her for her help, and ran home.

I needed my Thinking Chair. I went to the toolshed, plonked myself down, and propped my feet up on my tiny, overcrowded desk. I stared out the Plexiglas window at the rapidly fading daylight, and considered things.

Jeremy said he'd burned that disk yesterday, in the computer lab. Assuming that was true, the disk must have been ruined sometime during school yesterday. It couldn't have been damaged this morning, because the waterproof sealant whatsit had dried hard, and that would have taken a while.

So when could The Purple Avenger have struck? During lunch break? Possibly, but surely Jeremy would have noticed the disk was damaged, or at least missing, by the afternoon?

I called Izzy. "Could you get me a list of everyone stayed late after school yesterday? Apart from the staff; they'd have no motive."

"No problem. I'll have it for you in the morning," said Izzy.

Our principal is very keen on sticking to the rules. And Rule Number One in her rule book is "Nobody Is Allowed In School After Hours Without Permission." Not so much as an ant could wander the corridors without permission. Which, in this case, was good news for my investigation.

I sat in my Thinking Chair until it was nearly dark. By then it was getting cold outside, and I was getting hungry, but as I tried to leave, the door to the shed wouldn't budge. I realized Humphrey must have escaped again. I was pushing and yelling for twenty minutes before the wretched hound would move his fat behind.

SO! The Purple Avenger must have taken the disk from Jeremy's bag at school, covered it in that waterproof sealant stuff, let it dry, then put the disk back in the bag. IF Izzy's list shows that Jeremy stayed late, then that would probably be when The Avenger struck. (Because there would be a lot less people around who could witness the disk getting snatched.)

WHICH MEANS!
Izzy's list will also be a list of suspects! (Because everyone else would've gone home by the time The Avenger struck.)

BUT! If The Purple Avenger had to take the disk out of Jeremy's backpack ... Why not just steal it? Why risk getting caught putting it back? Why all The Purple Avenger stuff?

Unless the note is a fake clue, to throw the scent _off_ of Jeremy. Which would imply that Jeremy... did it himself.

It's looking more and more likely that Jeremy _did_ do it himself. For whatever reason. He _is_ our class's only reader of THE PURPLE AVENGER comics. Maybe he didn't want to hand in his essay because he thought it was bad? No, highly unlikely. Besides, nobody _needs_ to enter the competition, it's purely by choice.

FACT: I am very confused.

CHAPTER FOUR

On my way into school the next morning, I passed by the janitor's ladder. Once again, it was propped up beside the leaky roof over the bathroom. The janitor was slapping on the waterproof sealant whatsit with a huge, sticky-looking brush. And the sticky-looking bit was purple.

"Mornin', Mr. Gumm!" I called.

He gave me a nod.

"Er, Mr. Gumm," I continued, "you haven't, by any chance, possibly, maybe, had some of that waterproof sealant whatsit go missing, have you?"

He suddenly turned away from the roof and stared at me. "Yes!" he said. "A jar I'd just opened disappeared the other day. How did . . ? Hang on, was it you? It *was* you, wasn't it?!"

"No, I'm just a brilliant detective!"

"Oh yeah? Who's your teacher? What's your name? You thieving little monster! Hey, get back here!"

I ran out of there. Quick.

At least I'd all-but-confirmed what The Purple Avenger had used to purple that disk. However, as soon as I got to class, the happiness I felt at my own cleverness fizzled away like air escaping from a balloon.

The bell was about to go off. Mrs. Penzler was about to arrive. The entire class stood frozen to the spot, mouths gaping, staring at the large sheet of paper that Izzy had pulled from her desk.

Yesterday, this piece of paper had been covered in a complicated hand-drawn diagram. Today, it was covered in purple goo. And slapped into the center of the now-dry goo was a note, printed on top of a cut-out section of comic book:

THE PURPLE AVENGER STRIKES AGAIN! HA!

At that moment, the entire class gave the second in their trio of loud gasps. Izzy Moustique was furious. "That took me DAYS!" she wailed.

"Oh dear," smarmed Harry Lovecraft. "Looks like Moustique's out of the running, too."

I glanced at Jeremy Sweetly. He was trying so hard to look innocent that he might just as well have had *IT WAS ME! GUILTY!* stamped on his face. His cheeks were getting redder than a toddler's who's just done something nasty in his pants.

"Dear me," oozed Harry Lovecraft. "Looks like this Purple Avenger is getting the better of our class detective."

Everyone looked in my direction. "I'm following up on a number of important leads," I said grandly. I don't think they believed me. *I* didn't even believe me.

Izzy came over, holding out the ruined diagram. "Saxby, you've got to catch this person!"

"Are you really out of the competition?" I said.

"I can redo this sheet," said Izzy, "but it's going to take ages. I might not finish in time. Essays have to be handed in by the end of the week, remember."

"Did you get any info out of the note that was stuck on Jeremy's disk?"

"Not much. I can't tell exactly what comic book the paper came from, not without weeks of searching. The font that the message was printed in—and this second message, too, by the looks of it—is a standard one that's on all the school computers. And on half the computers in the world, probably. Actually, the word 'font' is incorrect. You should use the word 'typeface,' because in lettering a 'font' is—"

"Yeah, yeah," I said. "Okay, so the message is a dead end. Did you manage to get a list of everyone that was here after school the night of the first Purple Avenger attack?"

"Yup, no problem."

"I'll need a list of everyone who was here last night, too."

"Of course! You can cross-reference them. If someone was on both lists . . ."

"They had the opportunity to commit both crimes!"

I said. "That will narrow down the list of suspects even more."

Izzy spent that morning's recess in the school office, getting hold of all the relevant information. I spent that morning's recess dodging the janitor. He wanted his missing jar of waterproof sealant whatsit, and he wouldn't take "I didn't do it!" for an answer.

Once we were all back in class, Izzy gave me the lists. She'd thought ahead, and gotten hold of a list covering today (Wednesday) as well, just in case.

I checked through the lists while I sat gasping for breath. I'd run halfway around the school escaping that janitor. "I am so out of shape!" I wheezed to myself.

As I looked at the following lists, I was able to make an exact list of suspects: there were four people who could have committed both crimes.

Does your list match mine?

MONDAY LIST OF AFTER-SCHOOL ACTIVITIES

The following have permission to be on school premises.

DANCE GROUP Mrs. Womsey UPPER SCHOOL HALL	ANIME CLUB Mr. Nailshott COMPUTER LAB	BASKETBALL LEAGUE Mrs. Penzler LOWER SCHOOL GYM
Nina Suresh	Isobel Moustique	Scott Carey
Becky Wright	James McCrimmon	Anne Darrow
Jeremy Sweetly	George Mann	Michael Carpenter
Joanne Grant	Barry Sullivan	Laura Palmer
Nzinga Taylor	Alison Lethbridge	Matthew Ronay
Zoe Halibutt	Rob Blake	Harry Lovecraft
Vicki Waterfield	Li Chang	Jennifer Stannis
Liz Short	George Litefoot	Keith Avon
Sophie Tate	Henry Jago	Alex Garcia
Imogen Watkins	Emma Buller	Kathy O'Rac

TUESDAY LIST OF AFTER-SCHOOL ACTIVITIES

The following have permission to be on school premises.

ART CLUB Mrs. Vesey ART ROOM	SCHOOL PAPER Mrs. Clements COMPUTER LAB	FOOTBALL TEAM Mr. Hartright LOWER SCHOOL FIELD
Paulo Pesca	Jenny Maple	William Kemp
Isobel Moustique	Bob Bell	Jack Stapleton
Jeremy Sweetly	Maxine Dubin	Jonathan Small
Jasmine Winchester	Sophie Tate	John McFarlane
Anne Catherick	Netta Longdon	Charles Milverton
Percy Glyde	Harvey Bone	Isaac Fleisher
Laura Fairlie	Vicki Pike	Harry Lovecraft
Vincent Gilmore	Joe Stangerson	Henry Baker
Nicole Concepción	Lucy Ferrier	Alex Holder
Liza Michelson	Alice Turner	Susan Cushing

The list was:
- Jeremy Sweetly
- That low-down rat Harry Lovecraft
- Izzy
- Sophie Tate

Izzy didn't seem a likely Avenger. She'd been the victim of Purple Avenger attack number two, plus, if she was guilty, she'd hardly have left her own name on those lists for me to discover.

Sophie Tate was someone I hadn't considered. She wasn't part of my usual circle of friends, but as far as I knew, she certainly wasn't the type to start covering people's CDs and carefully made diagrams in purple goo. All I really knew about her was the fact that she always wore chunky shoes with great thick soles on them. And that didn't seem like a very helpful fact at all!

That low-down rat Harry Lovecraft was still at the top of the list, as far as I was concerned. I had no proof whatsoever, and nothing except my own suspicions to link him to The Purple Avenger. But these crimes were sneaky and spiteful, and anything sneaky and spiteful was Harry Lovecraft's specialty.

I checked the after-school list for Wednesday. There

was Jeremy Sweetly again on the list for Crafts Club. There, also, was Harry Lovecraft, down for Soccer Scrimmage, and Sophie Tate, who was on the swim team. But no Izzy. (Izzy would have been down for Chess Club, but they'd asked her to leave a couple of semesters ago—no one could beat her! She's still fuming about it.)

I was on the list too. Wednesdays were Book Club with Miss Bennett. That Wednesday was one I'd been looking forward to, because we were going to do detective stories, and I had plenty to say on the subject (having read our huge library of crime novels at home).

A brilliant idea popped into my head. At lunchtime, I did two things:

1. I apologized to Miss Bennett and said I'd be late.

2. I made sure I was within earshot of Sophie Tate, Jeremy Sweetly, and that low-down rat Harry Lovecraft, and talked loudly about how I was sure The Purple Avenger wouldn't dare purple *my* essay, which by the way was tucked safely away in *my* desk in the classroom.

95

I also had a quick word with Muddy. I needed his help, seeing as he's a genius inventor.

I'm sure you've spotted what my brilliant idea was?

Knowing that three of the four suspects on my list were going to stay late after school, I was hoping to catch The Purple Avenger red-handed (well, purple-handed). My own essay was going to be used as bait!

The split second the last bell rang, Muddy and I dashed for the door and headed to his house.

FACT: The Purple Avenger is now out to sabotage more than just Jeremy Sweetly!

I suppose I could just wait until The Purple Avenger knocks everyone out of the competition except him/herself. Then I'd know who it is.

But I wouldn't be much of a detective then, would I?

CHAPTER FIVE

"How about the Whitehouse Long-Distance Grab Mechanism Mark Two?" said Muddy, wide-eyed with enthusiasm. "I developed it from a rake and an old bike chain."

Muddy Whitehouse was a master at anything mechanical, but getting him to hurry up when he was around his inventions was like trying to move a boulder with a teaspoon.

"Muddy, no," I gasped, "thank you, no. I don't need any of that. I just need that video camera you said you've got."

It was ten minutes after school had ended. We'd dashed over to Muddy's place like a couple of rockets being chased by bigger rockets, and now we were in the garage attached to the side of his house (which is where he has his workshop). Or rather, as he likes to put it, his Development Laboratory.

The place was a junk shop. Covered in grime, littered with odds and ends, and full of half-finished ideas. Sort of like Muddy himself, come to think of it.

"Quick, quick!" I wheezed, still out of breath from the run. "I am sooo out of shape! I haven't got much time! Book Club is only an hour long, and I've still got to get back and put this camera of yours into position!"

"Ah!" cried Muddy, holding up a finger, as if a lightbulb had suddenly pinged into action above his head. "How about the Whitehouse Laser Cutter 2000?"

He dug through an old cardboard box and pulled out a device that was half fighter aircraft plastic model kit, half battery pack. "I adapted it from my mom's CD player. Of course, it doesn't actually cut things, as such. But there's a really cool little red light. Makes you look like a spy!"

"I'm not a spy," I said quietly. "I'm a detective. What on earth would I want a laser cutter for?"

"You *could* be a spy," he said hopefully. "I've got tons of great spy gear."

"I don't want spy gear, I want a video camera."

"Video cameras can be spy gear, too."

"Muuuuuuuddddyyy!" I cried through gritted teeth. "Camera! Please! Now!"

"Okay," muttered Muddy. "Your loss." He opened a small cupboard that had once been part of a kitchen, and took out a camcorder. It was small and light, and therefore ideal for my mission. It also had *Whitehouse VideoTron B* written in serious-looking letters on the side.

"The hard drive will store tons," said Muddy, "but you'll need to recharge the battery after an hour or so."

"That's fine," I said. "An hour is plenty."

"Of course, I rebuilt this thing from scratch. It dropped into some cranberry sauce last Thanksgiving, but I managed to get it all out."

"This is perfect! Thanks!" I shouted, already a hundred feet away and heading back to school.

When I got back to our classroom, I quickly checked to see if my essay was safe. Luckily, it was still untouched. The Purple Avenger hadn't struck yet!

Nobody was about. Which was lucky, since they

might have thought *I* was The Purple Avenger!

I placed the camcorder on the bottom shelf of the rack in the outside hall (where lunchboxes and sports equipment got dumped during the day). Here, it would be hidden from sight (unless The Purple Avenger was only about two feet tall), and would have a perfect view of the classroom and anyone entering or leaving it.

I set the recorder going. A tiny red light started blinking beside the lens. I gave it a quick wave and a grin, and hurried off to Book Club. I was still in time to amaze Miss Bennett and the rest of the club with the depth of my knowledge on detective fiction. Ta-daaa! The following morning, I could barely contain my giggles on the way to school. With a bit of luck, I'd be able to close the case in a matter of minutes.

I scooped up the camera while nobody was looking. Its battery had run down, and the light had stopped blinking. Nervously, I looked inside my desk. Had The Purple Avenger taken the bait? Was my essay now covered in waterproof sealant whatsit?

W-w-was it . . . ?

Yes!

I peeled the ruined remains of my essay off the top of my desk and held them up. Set into the middle of the goo was another one of those notes:

THE PURPLE AVENGER WILL ALWAYS WIN!

Everyone spun around and stared. At that moment, the entire class gave the third and last in their trio of loud gasps. After they'd finished gasping, they started talking in low whispers about keeping their work under armed guard from now on.

"Hang on a minute," I muttered to myself. "I've just spotted a flaw in my plan. Why didn't I put a *fake* essay in my desk . . . ?"

Making a muffled whining noise, I dropped the rubbery remains into the trashcan. Izzy gave me a look that was one-third sympathy, one-third horror, and one-third why-didn't-you-put-a-fake-essay-in-your-desk-you-silly-twit. Muddy gave me a big grin and a thumbs-up, and pointed at the camera.

That low-down rat Harry Lovecraft appeared at my shoulder, as if out of nowhere. He was smiling like a python in a box of mice.

"Tut-tut," he slimed. "This Purple Avenger has really

put one over on you, hasn't he, Smart? Tut-tut."

I tried to think of a witty comeback, but I couldn't. I was too busy seething with rage.

Muddy rooted around the candy wrappers in his pocket and produced a spare camcorder battery. "Thought you could use this," he said.

"Perfect!" I cried. "Harry Lovecraft will be smirking on the other side of his shiny face when he realizes I've caught him on camera!"

Quickly, I slotted the fresh battery into place and rewound the tape. While the rest of the class had moved on to talking in low whispers about keeping their essays in a bank vault until the end of the week, Iz and Muddy crowded beside me to view the evidence.

"Right," I said, pressing Play. "This is the moment when I prove what a low-down rat Harry Lovecraft really is."

On the camera's tiny flip-out screen, the video flicked into life. There was me, giving a grin and a wave at the camera . . . Aaaand I walk away . . . Aaaand we can clearly see the classroom door . . . Aaaand there's a long pause when nothing happens . . . Aaaand the picture goes *tzzzttt*.

"WHAT?" I cried. Suddenly, the screen was filled with a crackly fuzz. All you could see was a thin strip of floor at the bottom of the picture.

"WHAT?" I cried.

"Awww," said Muddy. "It's always doing that. I think the cranberry sauce must have damaged it more than I thought."

"WHAT?" I cried again.

"Camcorders are very complicated," said Muddy to Iz. "He's lucky it works at all. I offered him the Whitehouse Laser Cutter 2000, but ohhhhh noooo, he didn't want that."

They carried on their jabbering while I peered at the little screen, trying to pick out whatever details I could.

Suddenly, my heart gave a twitch. A shadow was appearing on the screen! Someone was sneaking into the classroom. I pressed Pause.

Almost all of the image was a blur, but in the thin clear strip at the bottom I could see a pair of ordinary brown shoes, tiptoeing.

And at that moment, I knew who it was. I didn't need to see their face on screen. By a process of elimination, I could work out which of the people on my suspect list was the guilty one.

My heart stopped twitching. It sank instead.

Have you figured it out?

It wasn't Izzy: she hadn't stayed late at school yesterday. It wasn't Sophie Tate: she wore shoes with thick soles. It wasn't Harry Lovecraft: his shoes were black and shiny. It could only have been Jeremy Sweetly.

The shoes on the video were rather stained and scuffed. Like a great slobbery dog might have chewed them here and there.

For the first time that morning, I looked over at Jeremy Sweetly. Or rather, I looked at his feet. Those shoes were unmistakable. I caught Jeremy's eyes. He could see what I was thinking, and I could see what he was thinking. He knew the game was up!

CHAPTER SIX

I had been totally wrong.

I simply *could not* believe it.

It really WAS him after all.

There *had* to be more to this than I was seeing.

At recess, I pulled Jeremy aside. He knew I knew.
And I knew he knew I knew.

"Jeremy, why?" I said.

He looked like he was about to cry. Which, to be
brutally honest, wasn't all that unusual for him. He'd
looked like he was about to cry when the class experi-
ment in growing lettuce had gone astray.

"Why?" I said again. "You're so sensible. And
sensitive. And . . . some other things beginning with
s. Why?"

He made a dramatic shrug. "Why not? I, umm,

er, umm, I was fed up with being sensible and sensitive. I thought I'd do something mean and nasty for a change."

"To your own work?"

"Yes. *That's* how mean and nasty I can be! Even my own work isn't safe! Yeah! Mmm. Mean and nasty, that's me," he said. He was completely unconvincing.

Then he said, "Are you going to tell Mrs. Penzler?"

"If I thought for one minute that you'd done it just to be mean and nasty, then yes, I would. But you didn't, did you? Who put you up to it, and why? Was it Harry Lovecraft?"

"No!" said Jeremy, rather too quickly.

I let the subject drop. Jeremy scampered away like a startled rabbit, clutching the latest issue of *The Purple Avenger* to his chest. He was scared, and it had nothing to do with being found out.

More than ever, I was sure Harry Lovecraft was at the bottom of this. But it wasn't simply a question of brute force. For one thing, Harry Lovecraft might have been sneaky and sly and underhanded, but he wasn't the sort of bully who went in for rough, head-down-the-toilet stuff. He was much too fussy about his shiny hair and his spotless clothes for that. He'd never dirty his hands by shoving little kids around on the playground.

And for another thing, Jeremy Sweetly was no fool. If someone had started pushing him around, he'd have said so. He knew that bullies were always cowards, just like the rest of us did. There was something else going on. Something was keeping his mouth shut. Someone had some kind of hold over Jeremy Sweetly.

But what? Harry Lovecraft had never had anything to do with Jeremy. They weren't friends, they had no friends in common, and as far as I knew, they'd hardly ever said so much as hello to each other. (In fact, now that I thought about it, the most that Jeremy and Harry Lovecraft had ever interacted was early last semester, when Jeremy caught him stealing someone's gym bag. Nothing unusual there. Izzy and I had reported him only a few weeks later, when he tried getting money off some younger kids by calling it "School Lunch Tax.")

Normally, people like Harry Lovecraft and people like Jeremy Sweetly just didn't bother with each other.

The two of them didn't even live in the same part of town. What possible connection could there be?

I needed Izzy's help again. I needed information. There had to be some kind of link I was missing.

"What kind of link?" asked Izzy, puzzled.

"Some kind," I said, looking all narrow-eyed and mysterious.

"And what if you're wrong?" said Izzy, doing a silly, bug-eyed impression of my mysterious look.

"I'm never wrong," I said.

But, I had to admit to myself, I could have been on a track that was more wrong than a Times Square shuttle train on the Hartford & New Haven line!

However, during the course of the day, I had two useful bits of luck. Two pieces of luck that would end up solving the entire riddle.

CHAPTER SEVEN

Piece of luck number one: a remark made by Harry Lovecraft while we were all returning to class after lunchtime. Jeremy Sweetly had stepped in a puddle with those battered brown shoes of his. Harry Lovecraft, noticing Jeremy giving his foot a shake to help it dry out, smarmed past his desk saying, "Hmm, Sweetly's in need of new shoes again. Why don't you get Humphrey under control, Sweetly? Stop him from chewing up the family footwear all the time, hmm?"

The deduction to be made from this comment didn't hit me at first. But then, as we all sat down and got out our science books, it smacked me right between the eyes like a cartoon anvil dropped off a cliff . . .

Even if Harry Lovecraft knew that Jeremy *had* a dog (and why would he even know that?), how would he know this dog's name, and that he kept "chewing up the family footwear all the time"? Those were strangely precise snippets of information for Harry to have. You don't generally get to know a dog's bad habits unless you also happen to know its owner, do you? Or unless you've at least *visited* the owner?

Oh man, I thought to myself. Harry Lovecraft *has been to Jeremy's house!* (That low-down rat's visited my street, and I never even knew it! Ewww!)

At first, this deepened the mystery even more. What in the name of Sherlock Holmes would Harry Lovecraft be doing at Jeremy Sweetly's house? But then came piece of luck number two.

Right after school, Izzy e-mailed me. *Here's a piece of luck,* she wrote. *I did a quick read of Jeremy's winning essay from last year*—The Life Story of My Dad, *remember? It provided some interesting background info.*

But that wasn't the piece of luck. The luck was that I did a search on the Internet and came across something very similar that I think you'll find establishes a clear link between Harry and Jeremy.

The "something very similar" was a Web page entitled *Our Sales Team*, devoted to half a dozen shinylooking people who all sold spare car parts.

Can you spot the connection?

Rachel Verinder
Matthew Bruff
Donald Lovecraft
Franklin Blake
Rosanna Spearman
Andrew Sweetly

"That's *it*!" I cried. "That's it!"

I didn't even need to retreat to my Thinking Chair for this one. I had all the answers.

The next day was handing-in-our-essays day. Everyone had their work ready and waiting at nine a.m. (Well, everyone except the victims of The Purple Avenger.)

Mrs. Penzler marched in. "I hope everyone's remembered their essay," she announced, scanning the class with her smoked glasses. "'I left it on the bus' and 'My baby sister ate it' are not acceptable excuses. Yes? Saxby?"

I'd raised my hand. "Could I have a word with the whole class, before we go any further?"

"Is this an excuse for not handing in your essay, Saxby?" sighed Mrs. Penzler.

"Umm . . . well, sort of . . . in a way," I said.

"Then, sorry, no," said Mrs. Penzler.

"But what if I could reveal The Purple Avenger's true identity?" I asked. "I can show that there's been cheating."

The class leaned forward, eyes wide. "Well, all right then," said Mrs. Penzler. "But you'd better be right."

I stood at the front, next to Mrs. Penzler's desk.

Everyone stared at me. Harry Lovecraft looked smug and confident. Jeremy Sweetly looked terrified.

I tried to give Jeremy a look that said, "Don't worry, I won't get you into trouble." But I really wasn't sure how to do that, so I think I ended up giving him a look that said "Just you wait and see," which I don't think reassured him very much.

"The identity of The Purple Avenger is . . . "

I paused for dramatic effect. The whole class leaned forward even more, eyes even wider. I couldn't pause for long, or eyes would've started falling out.

" . . . going to have to remain a secret."

The whole class groaned. Harry Lovecraft looked more smug and confident than ever. Jeremy Sweetly looked relieved.

"But!" I cried, one finger in the air. Everyone shut up. "The person responsible for The Purple Avenger attacks was *forced* to do what he did. Er, or she did. Umm, look, I'll call this person Person X, okay?

"Right. Person X purpled the work of Jeremy Sweetly, Isobel Moustique, and me. But Person X did *not* do these things voluntarily. Person X was being threatened. You see, Person X has a dog. A big, slobbery hound, which Person X loves beyond all reason. However, this dog is always wandering around the neighborhood. No matter what Person X does to keep him at home, the dog keeps escaping and getting himself into trouble. Now here's where Harry Lovecraft enters the scene . . . "

Everyone turned and stared at Harry Lovecraft. Mrs. Penzler said, "Saxby, you'd better be careful!" Harry Lovecraft didn't so much as twitch. He just gazed at me.

"Harry Lovecraft would normally have nothing to do whatsoever with Person X. But it just so happens that there is a connection. Not so much a connection between them, but a connection between their *parents*.

"It's a matter of public record—umm, I can't quite say *how* in Person X's case, 'cause that'll give away who Person X is—anyway, it's a matter of public record that Person X's dad and Harry Lovecraft's dad work at the same company, a company that makes and sells spare car parts.

"These dads both work in the Sales Team. One day they got together outside work. Harry Lovecraft's family went over to Person X's house. Harry Lovecraft and Person X, two people who normally would never, ever go anywhere near each other, were suddenly in the same social circle.

"So Harry Lovecraft gets to meet this big, slobbery dog. And he realizes that this dog is Person X's weakness. If he wanted to get Person X to do something, he wouldn't have to hit him or anything. Oh, no. All he'd have to do is drop nasty little hints about the dog getting out all the time, and about the dog maybe getting *lost*, maybe getting lost *forever*. You see what I'm getting at?

"So along comes the essay competition. Harry Lovecraft spots an opportunity. Person X is the favorite to win, and . . . Whoops."

I'd blown it. Everyone stared at Jeremy Sweetly. Jeremy Sweetly went redder than a sunburned tomato.

"Oh, man," I said. "Yeah, okay, it's Jeremy Sweetly. Let's move on. Sorry, Jeremy. Harry Lovecraft sees he can remove Jeremy from the competition by simply making threats about poor Jeremy's beloved dog.

"Now, this is where I went wrong. I assumed, as we all did, that The Purple Avenger was out to disqualify the people most likely to win. But that wasn't it at all. The competition had nothing to do with it. The competition was just a convenient opportunity. It was a matter of revenge.

"Last semester, you'll recall, Jeremy found Harry Lovecraft stealing someone else's gym bag. Naturally, Harry got into big trouble for it. The essay competition was Harry's chance to get even, as he saw it. Jeremy was the favorite to win. What better revenge, thinks Harry to himself, than to spoil Jeremy's chance at winning?

"But Harry Lovecraft, being Harry Lovecraft, can't just make Jeremy drop out of the competition and leave it at that. Oh, no. He wants his revenge to be a little more painful, a little more public. He's been to Jeremy's house, and he's seen that Jeremy reads The Purple Avenger comics. So Harry steals some sealant stuff from the school janitor, and he makes poor Jeremy destroy his own work, do it in the name of his favorite superhero, and show the world the results.

"You see, that was Harry's first mistake. The first of two. If he'd quietly made Jeremy miss out on the essay contest, we might never have known what was going on. Without the ruined disk, and the message, even I might not have suspected foul play. Harry might have continued making Jeremy's life miserable for ages. But no. Harry had to be Harry. He had to be cruel. In a way, he set up his own downfall.

"But at first, he got away with it. Nothing pointed to Harry Lovecraft as the guilty party. If anyone was going to get into trouble, it was Jeremy. So Harry gets greedy. Who else do I want revenge on? he thinks. Who reported him for his nasty little 'School Lunch Tax' scheme? Time for The Purple Avenger to strike Izzy's work, and mine. And if Jeremy gets caught, so what? If Jeremy starts pointing the finger at Harry, then all Harry has to do is make his threats all over again. Harry thinks *he's in the clear*."

Slowly, everyone turned to look at Harry Lovecraft. Now, Harry Lovecraft was looking extremely uncomfortable.

"So," said Mrs. Penzler quietly, "what was Harry's second mistake?"

"Oh, that's easy," I said, even more quietly. "He didn't figure on Saxby Smart."

For a moment or two there was total silence. Then Mrs. Penzler adjusted her glasses and barked, "Harry Lovecraft, Jeremy Sweetly, is this true?"

Harry had nowhere to hide. Now that his threats were out in the open, Jeremy had no reason to cover for him.

"Yes," said Jeremy, bravely.

"Yes," croaked Harry Lovecraft, through gritted teeth.

There was an uproar in the classroom. Once it had all died down, two things happened. First, Harry Lovecraft was sent to the principal's office. Second, Mrs. Penzler talked to the principal about postponing our handing in the essays until The Purple Avenger's victims could have a chance to redo their work.

"Thanks, Saxby," Jeremy said at lunchtime.

He gave me a sappy smile, and I think I spotted a tear in his eye, so I quickly said, "All in a day's work," and hurried off to talk to Muddy.

For the rest of the day, I felt pretty good about things. I'd solved a puzzling mystery, and everyone thought I was pretty cool. When I got home, I headed straight for my shed. I wanted to jot down some notes on the case while they were fresh in my mind.

Humphrey was flopped out in his favorite spot, right in front of the shed door. I spoke sharply. I spoke nicely. I whistled. I growled. I tried to tempt the drooling mutt away with a cookie. Nothing.

"Jeremmmmyyyyyy!" I yelled across the road.

Case closed.

CASE FILE THREE:
THE CLASP OF DOOM

CHAPTER ONE

There are some people you meet who simply make you smile. The kind of people who light up a room just by walking into it. The kind of people who make everyone around them feel happy.

Mrs. Eileen Pither is *not* one of them.

Legend has it she spent thirty-five years working in local government, turning orphans out into the street and counting stacks of coins in deep, dark dungeons. But all that was years ago. At the time of the case of *The Clasp of Doom*, she spent all her time organizing her retired friends and writing to the local papers about the terrible state of the roads, and how young people today have no manners.

Everyone in town knows Mrs. Eileen Pither. And Mrs. Eileen Pither knows everyone.

It was a wet, miserably gray day during spring break. A girl from the grade below me, Heather Gardens, called on me in my toolshed. She knocked, and the *Saxby Smart—Private Detective: KEEP OUT* sign dropped off the door, as usual. I made a mental note to get that thing nailed up properly once and for all, and sat Heather down on my desk. I flopped into my Thinking Chair and took up a steeple-fingered pose in order to look intelligent and detective-like.

"How can I help you?" I said. "Apart from doing your homework on plants, that is. But I'll leave that to you."

She blinked at me. "How on earth did you know I've been doing homework on plants?" she said.

"There are spots of green paint on your fingers, and the fresh Band-Aid on your left thumb shows you've got a slight cut there. Painting and cutting suggests making something. You're in the grade below me, which means you've very likely been given the same homework assignment over spring break that I was given last year. Which involved making a model plant. Bit of a guess, but I see I was right. Now, how can I help?"

Heather is a dark-haired girl with a slight build and a face dotted with freckles. At the time, her face was also dotted with worry.

"I'm related to Mrs. Eileen Pither," she said with a shudder.

Thunder rumbled overhead.

"I'm so sorry," I said. "I had no idea."

She shook her head, her eyes screwed up. "It's okay, really. I just don't talk about it, that's all. She's my mom's aunt."

"And she's caused some sort of problem, I presume? Is that why you're here?"

"Yes," she said. "You've heard how mean she is?"

"Who hasn't?" I muttered.

"She's accused me of stealing her jewelry. She's threatening to go to the police."

The thunder rumbled all over again.

CHAPTER TWO

"Give me the whole story, start to finish," I said. I leaned forward in my Thinking Chair. Rain spattered down the shed window.

"Mrs. Pither comes to our house every now and then. She keeps getting my mom to join organizing committees for various charities. Anyway, Mrs. Pither turned up to organize Mom last Saturday, and as she was leaving, she suddenly turned around in the doorway and pointed at me. 'Where is my antique clasp?' she demanded. I had no idea. She started getting angry, and said I must have stolen it."

"What does this clasp look like?" I asked.

"It's a hideous thing," said Heather, wrinkling her nose. "It's shaped like two hands, sort of curled around each other. They're made of silver, with little diamonds set into the fingers. There's a big, sharp, pin-type clip at the back. She uses it to hold the sides of her coat together, a ratty old thing."

"Yes, I've heard she is," I mumbled.

"No, the coat is a ratty old thing! It's green, and it stinks of mothballs. She's never without it. I think she's too cheap to put new buttons on it, which is why she uses that clasp."

"She had it when she arrived?" I said.

"Oh, yes," said Heather. "I saw it. Right there, clipped on at chest level. She thought I was admiring it! I kept myself busy in my room while she and Mom were talking, and I happened to come downstairs just as she was leaving."

"I presume the coat, with the clasp, was hanging up somewhere while she was with your mom?"

"Yes," said Heather. "In the hall. She put the coat back on, stepped out the front door, and then must have noticed the clasp was missing."

"And how long was the coat hanging in the hall?"

"About an hour."

"And *could* anyone have stolen it?"

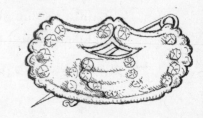

127

"Well, yes, I suppose someone *could* have taken it during that time. But apart from Mrs. Pither and Mom, only me and my older brother were in the house."

"Nobody could have snuck in?"

"Mom would have seen anybody coming to the front of the house from where she was sitting. And I would have seen anybody at the back because my room overlooks the yard."

"And I assume the clasp has been searched for?" I said.

"Everywhere!" cried Heather. "My mom and I turned the house upside down. There's no sign of it."

"You're sure she didn't lose it somewhere outside the house?"

"No. She definitely had it on when she arrived. It definitely wasn't there when she left. We even searched her nephew's car! She makes him drive her wherever she wants to go, because she can't drive herself. She gets what she wants out of him by playing the I'm-a-poor-feeble-old-lady card. He's softer than melted butter."

"He didn't come into the house?"

"No, he was off doing her shopping the whole time. He'd just arrived to pick her up."

I sat back in my Thinking Chair. "Very odd," I muttered. "I wonder why Mrs. Pither would assume it had been stolen? And stolen by you?"

Heather shrugged. "Because she's mean?"

"Hmm, yes, could be," I agreed.

"I think it's because she thought I was admiring it when she arrived. She's never liked me," said Heather. "Of course, she doesn't like anybody under the age of about a hundred and fifty. And now she's convinced I've taken this clasp of hers."

"Is it valuable?" I asked.

"I don't know," said Heather. "It doesn't *look* valuable. It looks ugly. I can't imagine anyone paying so much as a penny for that horrible thing."

"And you say Mrs. Pither is threatening to go to the police?" I asked. "Surely she has no evidence?"

"I think she's more interested in making a public fuss than anything else. Causing maximum embarrassment. It'll all go into motion first thing Monday morning, if the clasp isn't returned to her. She said to my mom, 'I'll give that girl until then to come to her senses and confess.'"

"And she'll really do it?"

"Without a shadow of a doubt," said Heather sadly. "She bursts kids' footballs if they land on her lawn, and she tried to sue her neighbors for having a barbecue. She's not going to think twice about getting me into trouble. She's already started gossiping to her committees about me. It's not fair! I'm really worried!"

"Never fear," I said. "Saxby Smart is on the case!"

FACT: The clasp definitely came _into_ Heather's house.

FACT: It was gone before Mrs. Pither _left_ the house.

FACT: They've looked for it _inside_ the house.

POSSIBILITY 1: It vanished into thin air. Hmm, not very likely.

POSSIBILITY 2: Heather really did steal it. Hmm, also not very likely. Why would she involve _me_, if she was guilty?

POSSIBILITY 3: Mrs. Pither's attempting some insurance scam! She could be pretending it's been stolen to get money out of an insurance agency.

POSSIBILITY 4: The clasp got dropped through a hole in the floorboards.

POSSIBILITY 5: Heather's older brother is involved. He's the only other person in the picture, but at the moment, I know nothing about him.

PLAN
I need to find out more about Mrs. Pither, this clasp, and Heather's brother. I also need to examine the scene of the crime...

CHAPTER THREE

I e-mailed my super-intelligent friend, Izzy, gave a detailed description of the clasp along with a rough sketch done by Heather, and asked her to track down whatever useful information she could find. I also made plans with Heather to visit her house the following day, so I could examine the scene of the crime.

The next day was the wettest and dreariest for ages; the kind of day when the clouds look like wet tissues, and the rain makes an endless roaring noise against the roof.

Heather lived in a very ordinary-looking house on a very ordinary-looking street. Rain drummed on the lids of the recycling bins put out all along the street.

When I arrived, I thought that the look of misery on her mom's face might be either dismay at the theft of the clasp, or else dismay at the horrible weather. But I was wrong on both counts.

"Mrs. Pither's on her way over," said Heather with a shudder.

"Excellent!" I cried.

Heather's mom looked at me like I was slightly mad. "Why, Saxby?" she gasped.

"Because I'd like to ask her some questions," I said. "If I'm going to investigate a—"

"Here!" interrupted Heather's mom, thrusting a duster into my hands. "Polish the bannister. She'll run her finger along it. If there's any dust, she'll make a sarcastic comment."

Heather whispered to me, "Mrs. Pither's got more committee stuff for Mom to do. My mom's too nice. If only she'd stop doing charity work around here, we'd only ever see that woman at major family events."

I polished the bannister. Heather swept the floors. Her mom tidied the living room and made sure there were the right number of cushions on the sofa for Mrs. Pither to sit comfortably.

While I polished, I took a close look at the hallway.

Beside the front door was a set of hooks, holding a couple of coats, a scarf, and a wool hat. Opposite the coat hooks was a small table, scattered with assorted keys, a couple pieces of mail, and reminders scribbled on scraps of paper. There was a little jar containing loose change, and a small pile of coupons for the local stores. Above the table was a mirror in a broad wooden frame.

The floors were made of that tough, wooden-looking stuff (so no holes in floorboards for clasps to drop into). The floor showed, as you'd expect, a faint pattern of scuff marks around the busy areas (with, I noticed with a smile, neatly rectangular untouched patches where nobody had walked, one beneath the table and a larger one under the coat hooks). The stairs, where I was busy polishing, began near the hall table, and a short corridor led to the living room and kitchen. Along the corridor hung three abstract paintings (a bit ugly, I thought) marked *TG* in the bottom right corners.

All very ordinary-looking. And not a single clue to be had from any of it . . . Or was there? I could tell that something was missing! How did I know?

I pointed to the coat hooks. "Something normally sits under those hooks, a box of some kind. There wouldn't be a big untouched patch of floor there otherwise. Not a neat, rectangular patch, anyway."

"Just the recycling bin," said Heather. "It's out on the curb right now—it's collection day."

"Ah!" I said. "Yes. I saw it on my way in. And . . . ?"

"Yeeees, it was searched," said Heather. "Mom searched it. Everywhere was searched."

Through the ripple-glassed panels in the front door, I could see a car pull up outside. Heather's mom bustled out of the living room. "Here we go," she mumbled. She took a deep breath and swung open the door.

Mrs. Pither was busy talking her nephew. He was supposed to go and pick up her new bureau from the furniture store, take it back to her house, put it together, and then come back to get her. The car pulled away quickly.

"Hello, Eileen," said Heather's mom.

Mrs. Pither was wearing the ratty old green coat that Heather had described to me, all threadbare and frayed at the edges. It flapped down to the level of her ankles, not because it was particularly long, but because she was particularly short. She clacked along in low-heeled shoes, her big feet duck-waddling at the end of sticklike legs. Her white hair seemed to have been gruesomely attacked with hairspray, and her face had the permanent look of having just drunk a glass of lemon juice.

"Morning," she barked, as if the word was rude. She spoke to Heather's mom, completely ignoring Heather and me. "Have you made enough people volunteer next week?"

"Yes, four," said Heather's mom.

"That's not enough," argued Mrs. Pither. "Here, hang my coat up, would you? Of course, I've been freezing in it, because I can't do it up, not since my clasp was stolen. Have you taken the collection boxes to the bank yet?"

"Yes, of course I have, Eileen. Now about—"

"Glad to hear it. You can't be too careful, what with thieves lurking around every corner. What's wrong with the heat? It's like ice in here."

She waddled along the hall to the living room, running a finger along the bannister and finding no dust. She made no comment. Heather's mom shut her eyes for a moment. "It's for charity," she muttered to herself. "It's all for charity . . . "

She whispered to us to go and make some tea, then followed Mrs. Pither. Heather and I scurried to the kitchen.

"Hmm," I said, getting out the cookies. "I'm surprised I'm not investigating a murder."

"Oh, she's in a good mood today," said Heather. "You should see her when she's annoyed."

The front door banged, and a few moments later Heather's older brother came rumbling along the hall and into the kitchen. It turned out he was eighteen years old, that his name was Tim, and that he was a student at the nearby college.

"H'lo," he said to me with a nod, dumping a handful of library books on the counter. He clunked about the kitchen making a sandwich. He was obviously one of those people who can't do anything without making a noise and leaving a mess. Even his shoes, and the bottom half of his jeans, were covered in multicolored spots that had clearly been there for ages.

"Did you hear about Mrs. Pither's clasp?" I asked him.

"Yeah," he said. "She prob'ly left it under her cat or somethin'."

As I picked up the tray of tea and cookies, I took a quick look at Tim's library books. Only one was turned so that I could see the title: *Costume Jewelry: Current Price Lists and Valuations.*

That was odd. Jewelry? Why would he want to find out the value of jewelry?

Unless he had the clasp, and wanted to see how much it was worth? Could *he* have stolen it?

He gathered his stuff and set off upstairs, chewing his sandwich. He dropped breadcrumbs and little splats of jelly as he went. As soon as he was out of earshot, I said to Heather, "Was Tim in his room when the clasp was stolen?"

"Yes, that whole afternoon," Heather replied.

Why? Why would Tim want to steal the clasp? Or, more to the point, need the money, since he was apparently trying to find out its worth? An idea struck me. Suddenly, I realized why he might be in particular need of cash.

"Tim spends a lot of money on stuff for classes, doesn't he? Stuff that gets used up?" I said.

"Yes," said Heather. "He owes Mom a small fortune. How on earth did you know that? I haven't even told you what he's studying."

Heather didn't need to tell me anything about what Tim was studying at college. I'd worked that one out already. Have you?

"He's studying art," I said. "There are abstract paintings hanging in the hall signed *TG*. That *could* be someone other than Tim Gardens, but the multi-colored dots all over his shoes and jeans are probably paint. What else would come in lots of colors? So he's an art student. And paint, canvas, brushes, and so on don't come cheap."

Heather smiled and shook her head. "Jasmine Winchester said you were always one step ahead. Anyway, why do you need to know what he spends on art stuff?"

I didn't think it was a good idea to tell Heather about my suspicions. Not yet. After all, suspicions aren't proof.

"Oh, nothing, just interested," I said. "Come on, let's take this tea in!"

In the living room, Mrs. Pither was organizing Heather's mom like a kindergarten teacher organizing a finger-painting session. Heather's mom kept scribbling notes in a thick pad.

I set the tray down on the coffee table in front of them. Heather's mom gave me a big grin that said "Thank you" and also "Help me, someone, she's driving me crazy." Heather quickly put the cookies on the tray and hurried out to escape Mrs. Pither. Mrs. Pither looked at the tray as if she'd ordered something expensive in a fancy restaurant and been served poop and tap water. I made myself comfortable. I wasn't going anywhere—I still had questions to ask.

"Is this tea freshly brewed?" snapped Mrs. Pither. "I'm a very delicate person. My innards can't take tea that's been allowed to stew in the pot."

"It's as fresh as a daisy that just this minute popped out of the ground," I said.

For the first time, Mrs. Pither looked directly at me. I flinched. It was like being stared at by a cobra.

"Who are you?" she said.

"This is Saxby, a friend of Heather's," said Heather's mom. "He's come over to help find this lost clasp of yours."

"Ah! Has that girl come to her senses yet? Has she confessed?"

"Eileen," said Heather's mom, pulling back her chin in a now-just-a-minute expression. "I've told you, Heather does not have your clasp. We're all very sorry it's missing, but—"

"I'm a very forgiving person," snapped Mrs. Pither. "If she returns the item with her express apologies, I'll only ask the police to give her a warning. But, as I have told you, if I don't get my clasp back by ten o'clock Monday morning, things will get a lot more serious!"

A bleeping sound thankfully drowned her out a bit—a truck was backing up, collecting the recycling out on the street.

"Mrs. Pither," I said. "Could I ask you a few questions about that clasp?"

"No you may not," she barked. "Who are you again?"

"Saxby."

"What a ridiculous name," she muttered.

I did my own bit of chin-pulling-in. "I'm investigating the disappearance of your clasp."

"Are you indeed?" she piped. "This isn't a silly game, you know. Run along home, you pest!" She started rubbing her ankle. It certainly looked rather sore. "My ankle has been bitten raw by insects for days! Does this sofa have fleas?"

"What?" cried Heather's mom. "Of course not!"

There was a distant bumping of plastic boxes from farther down the street, as the recycling bins were emptied. Heather's mom gulped down her tea to stop herself from saying something that would make her as rude as her guest.

"If I could just ask about this

clasp?" I inquired politely. "Did you have a handbag with you the other day? One the clasp could have been put into by mistake?"

"A handbag?" cried Mrs. Pither, her eyes stretching free of the wrinkles around them. "No, I did not! Do you take me for a fool, boy? My clasp was stolen by that girl!"

"I'm telling you, Eileen," said Heather's mom, "nobody in this house would steal anything!"

I said nothing.

"Well, someone in this house did," said Mrs. Pither.

"Mrs. Pither," I said, "did you go to the bathroom

while you were here? Or out into the backyard? I'm just trying to establish your movements."

Her eyes were on the point of dropping out and plopping into her tea.

"Honestly, Saxby," said Heather's mom, "we've covered all that. Heather and I searched the entire house, wherever Mrs. Pither had been or not."

"You did it between the two of you?"

"Yes, I checked the stairs, the driveway, the kitchen, and the hall. Heather did in here, the hall closet, the recycling bin, the coats and shoes, out back, in the—"

I leaped to my feet!

There had been a mix-up. Something *had* been missed!

"Oh *no!*" I yelled. I took a jump toward the window, realized I was wasting precious time, jumped

toward the door instead, and dashed out of the house. Heather, who was coming down the stairs, quickly followed me.

"What is it?" she called.

At that very minute, a garbage man was emptying the recycling bin from the hall into one of the big green containers that filled the back of the truck. My yell of "Stoooooppp!" was drowned out by the revving of the truck's engine. It rumbled away faster than I could run.

"But we searched the recycling bin!" said Heather.

"Who searched it?" I cried.

"I told you before. Mom did."

"Exactly! She just said *you* did. That bin was right below where Mrs. Pither's coat was hanging." I pointed wildly at the rapidly departing truck. "The clasp must be *on that truck*!"

CHAPTER FOUR

I had to think quickly! There was no way I could go back in the house and say, "Oops, sorry, Mrs. P., your antique jewelry is on its way for recycling."

Luckily, I'd spotted which green container they'd emptied the recycling into. My only hope was to intercept that container *before* it got emptied out.

I kind of skipped about for a second or two, not knowing what to do, looking like a complete idiot and making little "arg" noises. But then I had an idea.

"Muddy!" I cried at last. "Muddy lives on the next street!"

Leaving Heather looking bemused, I dashed over to Muddy's house. He was in his garage (otherwise known as his Development Laboratory), taking apart a broken DVD player.

"Muddy!" I gasped, almost tumbling over as I skidded to a halt.

"Hi, Saxby," he said, not looking up from his work. "Sorry, delicate operation. Whatever you do, don't knock my elbow."

"I need that bike you adapted, quick!" I wheezed. I added to myself: "And I've got to get more exercise."

"The Whitehouse Speedy 4000?" said Muddy, keeping his eyes fixed firmly on what he was doing. "Over in the corner. Why do you need it?"

"I'm on a case," I cried, grabbing the bike and the helmet that dangled from its handlebars. "I have to follow a truck."

Muddy suddenly looked up with a big grin on his face. The delicate piece of electronics he'd been examining toppled over onto the floor. "Ooh," he said. "You might want the Whitehouse Super-View Zoom Glasses, too? They're made from binoculars and a pair of my dad's glasses."

"No thanks."

"Or some Whitehouse Ultra-Headlamps?"

"It's broad daylight! How long do you think I'm

going to be chasing this truck? Sorry, GOT to go! I'll bring the bike back later!"

I sped away at top speed, before he could start going on about spy equipment. The Whitehouse Speedy 4000 had specially adapted gears: once you'd gotten it going (and that took an effort, because of the bigger cog-wheel-thingamajiggy beside the pedals), it flew along like lightning on its extra-chunky tires. Plus, it had pretty cool flame graphics painted on its sides.

The recycling truck was way out of sight. For a big truck, it was a fast mover; I'd seen it plenty of times in the past, rumbling along from street to street, hardly ever stopping, with garbage men dashing here and there collecting bins all around it. It was like worker ants feeding a giant queen with old newspapers and tin cans.

The trouble was, I didn't know what route it took. The roads in this area were a winding criss-cross of streets. It would be very easy to completely lose track of it. As I biked along, I strained to hear the echo of its engine. But the noise from the nearby main road made it impossible to pick out a specific vehicle.

I looked around for clues.

Of course! There was one very simple method of working out where the truck had (or hadn't) been . . .

I could track it by seeing which streets' bins had been emptied, and which ones' hadn't. Using this method, I caught up with the truck after about half a mile or so. Even then, I had to pedal like mad to keep up.

As I pumped my legs for all I was worth, two thoughts struck me:

1. I was glad my suspicions about Tim had been wrong. It would have been very unpleasant to reveal to Heather and her mom that there was a thief in their house after all.

2. I was going to have to search through a bunch of recycling to find this stupid clasp!

The things we detectives have to do . . .

I managed to keep up with the truck—just—until it headed for the recycling plant. I was finally able to get ahead of it, and was waiting there when it rumbled to a halt outside the gates, its brakes hissing.

"Hey!" called the driver. "You're not allowed past those gates, kid!"

I launched into my prepared speech. I told the men that I'd accidentally thrown away a treasured news-paper clipping about how I'd rescued a dog named Humphrey from drowning. (I didn't want to tell them the truth, just in case one of them got greedy and sent me packing so that he could find the valuable piece of jewelry for himself.) "Please, mister, please please

please, oh please, I know where it is, it's in that container there, Mister, please."

And so on, and so on. The garbage men looked at each other as if to say, "This boy is a complete idiot."

"Gooo on, then," said the driver. "Empty the bin over on the grass there. And put every last bit back. Got it?"

"Right! No problem! Thank you!" I said, beaming.

"Leave the bin by the gate when you're done. And don't be such a complete idiot in the future. I'm only letting you do this because of your being brave and saving that poor dog."

"Understood."

Once the gates had been opened and the

truck thundered through, I emptied out the green container.

The clasp was here somewhere, underneath all those old newspapers, tattered junk mail, ripped-out pages, and shredded paper. I wished I'd brought along some gardening gloves from my shed.

I set to work. I carefully turned over each and every piece of junk and then set it aside, making absolutely sure that nothing was missed, and that the clasp couldn't possibly stay undiscovered. After about half an hour, my hard work was rewarded . . . with precisely nothing.

The clasp wasn't there. It had never been in that recycling bin in the first place. I had been totally wrong.

FACT: The clasp wasn't lost in the recycling bin. And it can't be found anywhere else in the house.

CONCLUSION: It <u>must</u> have been stolen after all.

FACT: Tim is the only one on my suspect list.

AWKWARD QUESTIONS
How do I tell Heather?
How do I get proof?
How do I get the clasp back?
What if Tim's already sold it?
What will Mrs. Pither do when she finds out?

CHAPTER FIVE

Once I'd finished grumbling, griping, and putting everything back into the big green container, I did three things:

1. I pedaled back to Muddy's, returned the bike, and washed all the newsprint stains off my hands.
2. I went back to Heather's, told her that I'd been wrong about the recycling bin, and said my investigations would continue.
3. I went to Izzy's to see if she had any info for me.

"Not very much, I'm afraid," she said. "That clasp is . . . Are you listening?"

I was distracted for a moment. Since my last visit, Izzy had hung one of those disco ball things from her ceiling. The twinkling reflections almost made it look like her room was spinning.

"Sorry," I said. "Yes, I'm listening."

"That clasp could very well be pretty valuable," said Izzy. She consulted a set of printouts and adjusted her reading glasses on her nose. "Hideous, but valuable. From my research, I'd guess it's worth several thousand dollars. Items very similar to the one you described were made in the early twentieth century."

"So," I said, rubbing my chin detective style, "it would be worth stealing. Which is unfortunate."

"Why?" said Izzy. "Are you thinking Heather really did steal it?"

"Absolutely, definitely not!" I cried.

"Ooooh," said Izzy, flashing her eyebrows up and down. "I only asked! Could the great Saxby Smart be about to get a girlfriend?"

"Absolutely, definitely not!" I cried again. I gave her a hard stare. "As a matter of fact, I have a clear suspect, but I'm hoping I'm wrong on that score, too. I need more proof, or a whole new theory to go on. What about the Mrs. Pither insurance angle?"

"Well," said Izzy, checking her papers again, "it's not easy to say for sure, but from some old newspaper articles, I'd say Mrs. Pither is seriously rich."

"Really? And she goes around in that ratty old coat. She must make Scrooge look like a big spender!"

"I'm afraid it knocks your insurance scam idea out of the water," said Izzy.

"Yes," I sighed. "If she's well off, she'd have no need to try to fake her way into getting insurance money. Which points even more to a simple theft."

"'Fraid so," said Izzy.

Another thought occurred to me. "The thief would want to get rid of it quickly. The longer he held it, the greater his chances of being discovered."

Izzy snapped her fingers. "I'm one step ahead of you, as always! I've already checked all the sales and auction Web sites. Nothing."

"He might very well want to sell it on the sly," I said. "Keep an eye on those sites, I'll check around town. Heeey, hang on, what d'you mean, 'as always' . . . ?"

Once I got home, I went through the phone book and made a list of all the local shops and dealers who might trade in jewelry. I spent the rest of the day trudging around the shopping center, notebook in hand, asking one place after another if they'd been offered anything like the clasp. Nobody had. I also asked if they knew of any dealers not on my list who might be able to help me. Nobody did.

At each store, I used a cover story: I said that my dotty old aunt had mistakenly asked a friend to sell it for her. Honestly, she's soooo dotty, that aunt of mine! I said it was her *necklace* she'd meant to sell, and she was willing to buy the clasp back, if anyone had it. I needed a cover story because if any of the dealers *had* gotten the clasp, they might clam up if I started saying I was looking for something stolen. Or even if I said it was just plain lost—it could have been picked up in the street and sold by anyone.

My lack of success left me even more worried and confused than I'd been before. I retreated to my shed and sat in my Thinking Chair, feet up on the desk, staring out the shed window. It had started raining yet again, and droplets were thumping against the shed's wooden roof. I made a few notes:

Reasons for Thinking that Tim
Did It:

• He had the opportunity. Mrs. Pither's
coat, plus clasp, were hanging in the
hallway all that time. He was home.
Nobody ever checked on him.
• He has motive. He could definitely
use the money!
• Evidence: He had that book with
him. He was checking on prices, etc.

Reasons for Not Thinking that Tim
Did It:

• The clasp hasn't been sold. If Tim
needs the money and doesn't want to
get caught, you'd think he'd have sold
it as soon as he could. It wouldn't
make any sense not to sell it.
• In theory, Heather could still have
done it. Although, she doesn't have
the money motive that Tim does.
Unless I'm missing something . . .

However I looked at it, I had a big problem. It was noon on Saturday, and on Monday morning, Mrs. Pither would be turning up at Heather's house to cause trouble. In the meantime, as the saying goes, I was like a man with no toilet. I had nothing to go on.

What could I do to prove Tim's guilt? Or his innocence? If he still had the clasp—which seemed likely, since it hadn't been sold—the only thing to do was go through his room! And there was no way I could do that. I couldn't march into Heather's house, accuse her brother of being a thief, and ransack his bedroom. Could I?

But if I was *right*, I'd have revealed the culprit, with the dreadful side effect of causing a great deal of heartache for Heather's family.

But if I accused him and was *wrong*, my reputation as a detective would be in tatters. And Tim wouldn't exactly be my greatest fan, either. (Besides, Tim could have hidden that clasp in any number of locations—it wouldn't have to be his room. If that was the case, I'd be back to square one, *and* I'd have alerted him to my suspicions.)

Whether I was right or wrong, there was trouble

ahead. I sat back in my Thinking Chair, wondering if there was something I hadn't considered. Some little detail that would give me a few answers. Some fact about the events in Heather's house that would settle the question of Tim's involvement once and for all . . .

I almost leaped out of my Thinking Chair. Of course! There were three somethings that gave me the answer at last:

1. Something about the clasp itself.
2. Something about Mrs. Pither's penny-pinching habits.
3. Something about Mrs. Pither herself, that I'd noticed during my visit to Heather's house.

Tim WAS innocent. And so was Heather. I had solved the mystery!

Think back carefully . . .

CHAPTER SIX

Monday morning, nine-thirty. I was at Heather's house. (It was Teacher Training day!)

Tim was at class, Heather was sitting nervously on the living room sofa, and Heather's mom was pacing about, from hall to kitchen to living room to hall and back again.

"Are you sure about this, Saxby?" she said, as she passed through the living room on her way back to the kitchen.

"I promise you, I'm never wrong," I called after her. Her slippers flip-flopped up and down the hall.

"You'd better not be," said Heather quietly. "Because if you are, I'm in dead trouble in precisely . . . " She checked her watch. " . . . twenty-eight minutes."

"Relax," I said. "Got any more of those cookies?"

Twenty minutes later, a car pulled up outside, and there was a *ratt-ratt-ratt-ratt* at the door. Heather pulled her legs up under her on the sofa and gulped. After a few seconds, Mrs. Pither came swanning into the room and sat herself down in an armchair. I was pleased to see that she hadn't bothered to hang her ratty old green coat up in the hall. Heather's mom bustled in after her.

"Now then," announced Mrs. Pither. "I want my clasp returned, immediately and undamaged. I'm a very generous and understanding person, so I'm prepared to involve the authorities only to the minimum extent in this case, provided my clasp is placed in my hands right now. And before you ask, no, I will not accept a check. It is an heirloom. Its value is immaterial."

Her baleful gaze swept across the room, like a leopard sizing up its prey. "Well?" she barked.

"Eileen," said Heather's mom, after a deep breath. "We've been patient about this, because we realize it must be distressing to—"

"Are you claiming that you *don't* have my clasp?" cried Mrs. Pither.

"Of course we don't!" cried Heather. "We've been telling you that all along!"

Heather's mom held a hand out toward Heather, as if to say, "It's okay, don't lose your temper."

"Saxby here says he knows what happened to your clasp," said Heather's mom.

Mrs. Pither looked at me. I shuddered. "The boy with the ridiculous name?" she piped. "You stole it?"

"No," I said. "But I can, as you put it, place it in your hands."

"Then do so, you nasty little boy!"

"But first," I said, being really, really calm, "I think it's only fair that you apologize to Heather."

"I *beg* your pardon?" screeched Mrs. Pither.

"Surely, if I can prove that Heather had nothing to do with the disappearance of your clasp, the least she deserves is an apology?"

Mrs. Pither looked as if she'd just chewed up half a dozen hot peppers and was trying not to show it. I decided it was time for a full explanation.

"This case rests on a couple of small details. Details that might have been overlooked, if not for a third small detail. Like you, Mrs. Pither, I assumed that the clasp had been stolen, because it was clearly nowhere to be found. At first, I thought the culprit was Tim, for various reasons we don't need to go into at the moment.

"However, once I'd worked out the truth, I could also guess what Tim was up to. He was doing exactly what I was doing—investigating the matter. He was finding out about the clasp because he'd wondered, like I'd wondered, if Mrs. Pither was trying to pull off some sort of insurance scam."

"I *beg* your pardon?" repeated Mrs. Pither.

"But I'm only making a guess there. I guess maybe

Tim reached a dead end in his inquiries," I continued, "because he hasn't been around to notice these three details I mentioned.

"Detail number one: the clasp itself. Heather described it to me as having a big, sharp pin-type clip at the back. In other words, it's something that can give you a bit of a jab when it's undone.

"Detail number two: Mrs. Pither's coat. Now, Mrs. Pither is clearly a lady who is careful with her cash. Nothing wrong with that, of course. But that coat of hers has, if you'll pardon my saying so, seen better days.

"Detail number three: when I was here the other day, Mrs. Pither complained about her ankle. She said it had been bothering her, and she kept rubbing it. She thought it had been bitten by insects. She even made delicate, polite inquiries about whether that sofa there had fleas.

"There's nothing unusual about someone getting a few bug bites, is there? Except that it's hardly bug weather, is it? It's been wet, cold, and miserable for days. And why only bite her on one ankle?

"Taking into account detail number one and detail

number two, this third detail solved the puzzle for me. The clasp was not stolen. The clasp was not even lost, not strictly speaking. Why? Because, while the coat was hanging up in the hall out there, the clasp fell off. Perhaps Mrs. Pither hadn't done it up correctly; it's impossible to say.

"It didn't drop to the floor, or into the recycling bin. It fell into the lining of Mrs. Pither's old and ratty coat. That coat is frayed at the edges, and clearly threadbare. An object with a sharp point on it could easily get hooked onto something so worn. It didn't get hooked on the outside of the coat, or it would have been spotted. So it must have gotten hooked on the inside.

"And the clasp was, of course, still undone. Its point was sticking out, and poking through the material of the coat. We can even, er, 'pinpoint' the clasp. Mrs. Pither never goes anywhere without that coat, and as she walked, the point of the clasp scratched her ankle. She thought she'd been bitten. Now, if I'm right, Mrs. Pither, you've had the clasp yourself all along. Could you stand up, please, and raise the left hem of your coat?"

"I *beg* your pardon?" piped Mrs. Pither. "I've never heard such nonsense in all my life! As if I would be so careless as to leave a valuable clasp undone! As if I can't tell flea bites from the scratching of a pin!"

"If you could just go along with Saxby, for a moment?" said Heather's mom. "We'll soon see if he's right or not."

Mrs. Pither snorted crossly and stood up. She bent, took the hem of her coat between thumb and forefinger, and lifted it up so that its bottom edge was upside down.

Nothing.

"Give it a little shake," I said.

She gave it a little shake.

Clunk!

The clasp hit the floor, its pin wagging like a dog's tail. It was indeed an ugly piece of jewelry. Tiny gems glittered along the fingers of two silver hands, one gripped around the other.

Mrs. Pither stood there, staring at it. Heather and her mom stifled their laughter. I cleared my throat.

"So, umm, Mrs. Pither," I said. "Was there something you were going to say to Heather?"

Mrs. Pither suddenly snatched the clasp off the floor and pocketed it. She glared at the three of us, stone-faced, as if we'd just caught her washing her undies in the sink. She looked at Heather.

"I . . ." There was quite a long pause. " . . . owe you an apology," she barked at last.

She marched out of the room, and out of the house. Then she realized she'd ordered her nephew to drive to the post office, and marched back inside while she called him.

Meanwhile, in the living room, Heather and her mom took turns hugging me. Tim returned home a little later, and Heather made him drop his sandwich in surprise when she asked how his investigation was going.

I returned to my toolshed to make a few notes. I sat

back in my Thinking Chair, my feet up on the desk, and felt pretty good about things in general.

Case closed.

GOFISH

SIMON CHESHIRE

What's your favorite childhood memory?
Reading, in bed, before going to sleep at night.

As a young person, who did you look up to most?
Spider-Man. No, really, Peter Parker in the '60s and '70s Marvel comics was an object lesson in battling through against the odds. I wanted his courage and determination.

What was your worst subject in school?
Anything sports-related. Still gives me the shudders, even today.

What was your best subject in school?
History and English.

What was your first job?
Cleaning offices at 3 AM (when I was a student).

How did you celebrate publishing your first book?
By writing another one.

Which of your characters is most like you?
Probably Sam, the main character in *Bottomby*. Saxby Smart is very much the kid I'd like to have been: He's quite like me, but he has a self-confidence I never had at that age.

Are you a morning person or a night owl?
Night owl, definitely. Hate getting up.

What's your idea of the best meal ever?
My wife cooks the most wonderful chocolate and lemon pudding. Any meal which includes that is OK by me.

Which do you like better: cats or dogs?
Neither, I'm allergic to both. Seriously.

Where do you go for peace and quiet?
I'm not sure I've ever actually found it. . . .

What makes you laugh out loud?
The wide-mouth frog joke. Always makes me smile, always cheers me up.

Who is your favorite fictional character?
Me.

What are you most afraid of?
There are so many things that frighten me senseless, I wouldn't know what to choose. Bacteria, probably.

SQUARE FISH

What time of year do you like best?
100% summer. Don't like cold, don't like rain. And I live in England. Help.

What's your favorite TV show?
Of all time? *Doctor Who*, 1966–1978.

If you could travel in time, where would you go?
Into the future. I'd love to see how things turn out for the human race!

What do you want readers to remember about your books?
That they made them laugh. And the titles, so they can recommend them.

What would you do if you ever stopped writing?
Spend all day reading.

What do you like best about yourself?
I'm still alive.

What is your worst habit?
I'd say immodesty, but to be honest, I'm so close to perfect I don't think that counts.

What do you consider to be your greatest accomplishment?
My children.

Where in the world do you feel most at home?
In a world of my own.

What do you wish you could do better?
Write.

What would your readers be most surprised to learn about you?
I'm good at repairing computers.

R. W. ALLEY

What did you want to be when you grew up?

That depends on when the question got asked. In third grade, I wanted to be an astronaut or a clown. In sixth grade, I wanted to make puppets and put on shows. In middle school, I wanted to be a space explorer and make puppets. (I was done with the clown thing.) In high school, I wanted to fit in. In college, I thought I might be an art historian or make puppets and puppet movies. (The astronaut thing turned out to require some engineering skill and a strong stomach. It looked so much easier on TV.) Then one day, drawing a cartoon for the school newspaper, I thought, "Maybe I could do this for money." A wild notion, if you'd seen my drawings then.

I told my parents that I was going to be a lawyer.

When did you realize you wanted to be an illustrator?

The summer after college, I wrote and drew a story for fun. I thought it looked like a children's book, maybe. I showed it to a publisher and they bought it. It appeared that I had a career, or at least a job. The law would have to wait.

What's your first childhood memory?

Hard to tell. I've made up too many stories about what I seem to be thinking in my baby pictures.

What's your most embarrassing childhood memory?
(See above.)

What's your favorite childhood memory?
When it was very quiet on Saturday mornings, I'd sit at a little table in front of a small black-and-white TV and make clay figures and make up stories for them while I watched *Captain Kangaroo, Top Cat,* and *Fireball XL5.*

What was your worst subject in school?
Languages have always confused me.

What was your best subject in school?
History and English. My junior high and high school had no arts programs (visual or performing). It wasn't until college that I took an art class. I wasn't very good at it. I could never finish anything. I just kept doing the same project over and over.

What was your first job?
I sold televisions at a local department store. I was not gifted at sales. And the store is no more. Coincidence? You judge.

How did you celebrate publishing your first book?
I forgot to celebrate. I was in the middle of working on a second book.

Where do you work on your illustrations?
In a very nice room that used to be the garage but now has a tall bookcase with a rolling ladder.

Where do you find inspiration for your illustrations?
Everything around me provokes a visual idea. I love architecture and faces. I am always looking and trying

to remember what I see. A very useful skill for an illustrator.

Are you a morning person or a night owl?
I am a morning and a night person. I find the afternoon the most useless for working. Of course, this may be because I am sleepy.

What's your idea of the best meal ever?
Lobster in a restaurant beside the dock where the boat that earlier in the day hauled in the trap that caught my lobster is tied up.

Which do you like better: cats or dogs?
I like the loud variety of dogs and the quiet elegance of cats.

Where do you go for peace and quiet?
Inside my head

What makes you laugh out loud?
My children, my wife, most Monty Python and a good fart joke

What's your favorite song?
"Try to Remember" from the musical *The Fantasticks*

Who is your favorite fictional character?
Toad, Ratty, Mole, and Badger from *The Wind in the Willows*

What are you most afraid of?
A bad fart joke

What time of year do you like best?
No time of year. Time of day. Early morning and just before midnight.

What's your favorite TV show?
No favorite. None are that consistent.

If you were stranded on a desert island, who would you want for company?
My wife and children. Although, if we don't get a good cell signal, I'm not so sure about the children.

What's the best advice you have ever received about illustrating?
My advice has come from the drawings of the illustrators/artists I admire most: "Make it simple, make it clear, and don't overwork it."

What do you want readers to remember about your books?
Mostly, that they remember them.

What would you do if you ever stopped illustrating?
Do you know something I don't?

What do you consider to be your greatest accomplishment?
My children and a happy marriage

Where in the world do you feel most at home?
In my home

What do you wish you could do better?
Draw horses. I really stink at drawing horses. Also, shoes. Not so good on shoes.

What would your readers be most surprised to learn about you?
Next to lobster, I think an anchovy pizza is the best meal.

A very valuable comic book has been stolen.
There might be a treasure hidden in The Horror House.
Six houses seem to have been searched by a dangerous intruder.

SAXBY SMART
Private Detective

in
TREASURE
OF
DEAD
MAN'S
LANE
and
Other
Case Files

Simon Cheshire
Pictures by
R.W. Alley

Saxby's got three more cases to solve and he needs your help in

THE TREASURE OF DEAD MAN'S LANE
and Other Case Files

CHAPTER ONE

I'm not very good at making things. Whenever I put together one of those do-it-yourself models (you know, fighter planes, sports cars, etc.), it always ends up covered in globs of glue. And with a piece stuck on backward. And another piece that falls off as soon as I put the "finished" model on my shelf.

So I should have known better than to try to fix my Thinking Chair. As readers of Volume One of my case files will know, my Thinking Chair is a vital part of my work as a brilliant detective. It's a battered old leather armchair, and in it I sit, and I think, and I mull over important facts regarding whatever case I happen to be working on.

My Thinking Chair had developed a small rip in one of the arms. One afternoon during Spring Break I

was in our toolshed trying to patch it up with a piece of super-tough heavy-duty fix-it tape. *Guaranteed 100% Bonding Power!* it said on the roll. The trouble was, it was 100 percent bonding my fingers together.

Just as I was wishing I'd asked my very practical friend Muddy Whitehouse to do the job for me instead, there was a knock at the shed door. Immediately, I heard the sign fall off (the sign I keep nailing up outside, which says *Saxby Smart—Private Detective*) and sighed.

"Come in!" I called.

In walked Charlie Foster, a boy who's in my grade at school. He's an owlish kid, the kind of person who gives the impression of being chubby even when he's not. He wears tiny round glasses and has a habit of sniffing a lot.

He looked around the cluttered shed. Half of it, as always, was packed with old yard equipment and random tools and things belonging to my dad (I'd found that super-tape in one of his piles). The other half of the shed was crammed with my desk, my files, and my Thinking Chair.

He handed me the sign. "Hi, Saxby. This yours?"

You can tell he's not the
sharpest nail in the toolbox,
can't you? He was looking
a little scared, and holding
a slightly crumpled, hand-
written note.

"What can I do for you,
Charlie?" I asked. "Who
told you to come see me?"

He sniffed in amazement.
"How'd you know it wasn't my idea?"

"People who need my services don't usually show
up looking like they don't want to be here," I said.
"Besides, that note you've got there is written in an
adult's handwriting. My guess is that someone's given
you specific information to take along."

"Well, yeah," said Charlie, with another sniff. "My
brother, Ed. He's nineteen."

"And why does your brother, Ed, need my help?"

"His comic was stolen."

My eyes narrowed. "Hm. Yeeees, I can see that that
would be annoying. I don't want to sound rude here,

but, um, wouldn't this be filed under Not That Important? Or maybe, I'll Go Get Another Copy?"

Charlie suddenly seemed to remember the note, and he smoothed it out a little and double-checked some of the writing. "The comic's worth a hundred thousand dollars."

CHAPTER TWO

"How much?" I gasped. "What's it made of, solid gold?"

I fell back into my Thinking Chair. This made the rip even worse, but right then I was only concerned with hearing more about Charlie's problem. Or rather, his brother, Ed's, problem. Charlie blew the dust off an ancient crate of paint cans and sat down.

"Ed collects comics," said Charlie. "He buys and sells them, and he's got shelves full of really old ones, worth a lot."

"Seeing as it's the middle of a weekday, and he's sent you instead of coming himself, I deduce he usually has to be somewhere right now. So trading comics is his hobby, not his job?" I said.

"Yes, that's right," said Charlie. "He works at that

restaurant on Church Street. He's a chef. But he's hoping to trade comics full-time. Or he *was*, until this comic got stolen."

I settled deeper into my Thinking Chair, trying to ignore the low ripping noise coming from its arm. "So . . . Tell me all about this comic, and what exactly has happened."

"It's the first issue of *The Tomb of Death*," said Charlie. He consulted Ed's note again. "Published in 1950. Only a few thousand copies were printed, and there are less than six still known to exist."

"And what's so special about the first issue of *The Tomb of Death*?"

"Dunno, never read it." Charlie shrugged. "But comics collectors dream of owning a copy. It's one of the most valuable comics in the world, Ed says."

"And when was it stolen?" I asked. "Give me every detail you can."

"Ed keeps it . . . er, kept it . . . in our wall safe. Dad had the safe put in because sometimes he keeps a lot of cash in the house, if he can't get to the bank after his store's closed. But Ed uses it the most. *The Tomb of Death* was in a see-through envelope, propped up against the back of the safe."

"And how long had it been there?"

"Ed inherited it a couple of years ago. Our grandfather was really into comics as a kid, and when he died, he left Ed two big boxes of old comics. And one of them was *The Tomb of Death*."

"It was always kept in the safe?"

"Always. Ed hardly ever took it out. It was way too valuable for that, and delicate too. It stayed in the safe twenty-four-seven!"

"Why didn't Ed sell it?"

"I think he was going to. But I'm not sure, you'll have to ask him."

"And when was it stolen?"

"Last weekend. Dad opened the safe on Monday morning, and it was gone."

"Just like that?"

"Just like that."

"Someone cracked the safe? There'd been a break-in?"

"Ed and Dad say no. We have an alarm system, and

it was never triggered. The safe's got an alarm, too, and that didn't go off, either."

"Was it in there on Sunday?"

"Yup. Dad had put his store's weekend earnings in there. The comic was still in the safe then. Definitely. I saw it myself."

"So there'd been a lot of cash in the safe that night?"

"Yeah. That's why the safe was opened up Monday morning—so Dad could take the money to the bank."

Two important clues had already become clear to me. One of them was about the safe, about *how* someone had gained access to the comic. The second important clue was about the comic itself, about *why* the thief had stolen *that*, instead of the money that was there too. Can you work out what I was thinking?

Clue No. 1: If two alarms weren't triggered, and no burglar was involved, then the safe was almost definitely opened by *someone who knew the combination*!

Clue No. 2: If the thief took an old comic but left a pile of cash untouched, then the thief was almost definitely *someone who knew how valuable the comic was.* They knew it was worth more than that pile of cash!

"This is quite puzzling," I mused. "Didn't Ed go to the police?"

"They said there's nothing they can do about it. There wasn't a break-in or anything. It's like the comic just vanished into thin air, overnight."

I stood up decisively. "Okay, these are there two things I'm going to do, in reverse order: No. 2, I'm going to examine the scene of the crime; No. 1, I'm going to try and get this awful super-tough, heavy-duty tape off my fingers. Tell your brother that Saxby Smart is on the case!"